THE SHINING MOUNTAINS MYSTERY
by Patricia Pomeroy Tanner

For if you forgive men when they sin against you, your heavenly Father will also forgive you. But if you do not forgive men their sins, your Father will not forgive your sins.
Matthew 6:14-15 NIV

To Debbie
God bless
Patricia Pomeroy Tanner

This book is dedicated to my grandparents, William Augustus and Mary Helena Pomeroy. In 1894 they journeyed by covered wagon from Minnesota to Livingston Montana, where my father Elmer was born on January 7, 1895. Six months later they once again hitched up the wagon and moved on to Kalispell, Montana where they settled.

Although this is a book of fiction, my desire was that it to be realistic as possible, so I enlisted the aid of my niece Sandi La Salle and her husband Patrick, former Montana ranchers. They helped me to be as accurate as possible about ranch life, the flora, fauna and the terrain where this story takes place. Sharon Sandman, also my niece, assisted me with important information. Her late husband Dick was the Chief of the Fire Management Bureau for the Department of State Lands Division of Forestry for the State of Montana. He was responsible for setting up fire caches that contained a water tanker, pulaskis and shovels in strategic areas that were readily available to the ranchers in case of a range fire. My editor, Denise Padgett, worked patiently with me through rewrites and revisions. And my friend Dell Collins furnished me with needed data about the San Diego area. To all of you, I give my thanks.

THE SHINING MOUNTAINS MYSTERY

Chapter 1

A large palm tree shaded the patio where Charity Wayne was stretched out on a recliner, reading a book by one of her favorite authors. She was temporarily distracted by the sound of her mother's car as she parked it in the driveway. Then, once more absorbed in her book, Charity paid no attention to the slam of the front door, the buzz of Jean's cell phone, the brief conversation and the click of her mother's heels on the kitchen tile. However she looked up at her mother when she came out the back door.

"You look comfy," Jean stated as she took the chair next to her. Jean's dark brown hair, fashioned in a modern coiffure, framed her heart shaped face.

Charity slipped a marker in place and laid the book on a nearby patio table. "I was just trying to unwind a little before dinner."

"Rough day?"

"Extremely, we seem to get most of our more difficult animals all on the same day. Today was one of those times."

Jean stood, her large brown eyes widened as she scrutinized her daughter. "You didn't get bit or clawed, did you?"

"I'm fine, just tired."

"I...uh...have something to tell you." Jean said after a pause, changing the subject.

Charity didn't miss the hesitation in her mother's speech pattern. Turning she studied her. "You seem nervous. It must be serous."

Jean sat back down and started tapping her foot, an anxious habit that annoyed Charity. "Uh...it is and I don't know how you're going to take it."

"Mom, please stop tapping your foot."

"Oh...I didn't realize that I was doing it." She pulled her feet back together and under the chair.

"Now tell me what you have to say. For heaven sakes, we have always been able to talk."

"I know but..."

"But nothing." Charity rose, then turned to face her mother. "Out with it."

Jean sighed and took a deep breath. "Well you know I have been going to church with Judy and last week, at the service, I became a Christian." She stated. A frown of apprehension creased her brow.

"What's wrong with that?"

"Nothing...I mean...well... I have been keeping something from you and after last evening...

"Your conscience got to bothering you, Right?"

"Yes. I think the Lord has been working on me."

"What did you do Mom? Buy something you shouldn't have or plan a trip without me?... I know...I know...You have a new boyfriend!"

"No."

"I bet that's it. You've been keeping him a secret. You've finally met Mister Right! And those nights out with the girls weren't really nights out with the girls." She clapped her hands together.

"No! Listen to me," she pleaded.

Charity looked intently at her. "Okay, what is it?" Then she sighed and rolled her eyes up. "You're tapping again."

. "Oh sorry."

"Why don't you just say it and get it over with."

Jean stood and walked to the edge of the patio. A belt of pink and red geraniums, heavy with blossoms, bordered it on three sides. Carpets of green grass spread out in every direction. A wooden, red and white birdhouse, made by a local craftsman, rested on a twelve foot white pole that stood at the end of the patio just beyond the flowerbed. Its inhabitant, a little Yellow Warbler had taken refuge there, waiting for warmer weather when he would take wing and journey north.

Jean turned, clenched her fists and said between her teeth, "Well here goes...I told you that your father died before you were born."

"So."

"That's...that's not true..."

"What!" Thunderstruck, Charity sat down.

Jean spoke in between little short breaths. "Uh...he's...alive...he's a...rancher...in Montana."

All Charity could do was momentarily,

speechlessly gape at her mother.

"I...knew that uh...he would want to see you...uh to be part of your life and I didn't want to send... you back and forth to Montana."

"So you're telling me that he doesn't know about me," she said, with a counterfeit calmness. Emotions were rushing through her, all mixed up together, shock, anger, frustration and sadness. Also a familiar feeling of deep down longing that she had felt all her life for the dad she never knew.

"No... I was.... about two months pregnant... with you... when I left him." Tears were streaming down Jean's face. She made no effort to wipe them away.

Charity didn't speak for a moment. Then she started screaming at her mother. "How could you? I wanted a dad so badly! I begged you to marry one of the men you dated. I felt so unbalanced!"

"Charity I was wrong! Please... forgive me!"

"Never!... I will never forgive you!" She dropped her face into her hands and started to sob.

Jean walked over and put her arm around Charity's neck but before Jean could say anything more, Charity knocked it off and jerked away. It was Jean's turned to be shocked "I... should have... told you as soon as you were... old enough to understand."

"But you didn't! Did you? ...Weren't you a little bit bothered by your deception?"

"Uh...no. You see, it was only after I excepted Jesus as my Savior and He started working on my heart, that I knew I had to make things right."

Charity stared at her mother, nonplussed. Neither spoke for some time. "I don't understand," she said finally.

"Well when I accepted Jesus. I gave myself to Him. He's the Son of God and it says in the Bible which is the holy word of God that we're not to lie to one another."

Charity stopped pacing. "So now all of a sudden you're Miss Goody Two Shoes!" she sneered.

Jean said nothing as she sadly studied her daughter.

"Where in Montana is my father's ranch?" she demanded after a pause.

"It's a little west of the center of the state. It's next to the Missouri River."

"How can I reach him?"

"I have his address."

"Get it for me."

Charity had never talked to her in that tone of voice before and Jean would never have allowed it under normal circumstances but she over looked the infraction because of the emotion involved and went to get the address.

"Why did you leave him?" Charity asked, after her mother returned and handed her the information.

She watched Charity shove the paper into her pocket. "I guess I wasn't strong enough to be a rancher's wife."

"Didn't you love him?" She asked, with a sob.

"Yes of course...but things got in the way. It's hard to explain."

"What you mean is, you cut and ran when things got tough."

"Something like that."

Charity scowled at her mother then she turned

away. "You make me sick!" Without another word she jerked the back door open. Sobbing she hurried to her room, grabbed her purse and flew out the door.

Jean followed her. "Charity, Charity!" she called out in vain as Charity jumped into her car and raced off down the street.

She drove around for hours. Finally she was thinking clearly. Charity drove home, parked in front and walked across the lawn. Her mother looked up from the couch when Charity came through the door. She could see the pleading in her mother's eyes. Briefly they looked fixedly at each other. Then with resolve, Charity marched into her room, packed a bag and marched back into the living room. "I'll get the rest of my things tomorrow," she said curtly.

"Where are you going?" Jean's eyes were floating in tears.

"To a motel tonight."

"Then what?"

"I'm not sure. I just know I am not going to live under the same roof with you."

Jean gasped but didn't say anything.

Charity left.

Later, from a motel, Charity called her partner Dr. Elrod Lake and told him that she needed a couple days off.

"I guess I can handle it, but if things get crazy, you'll have to come in and help," he grumbled.

"Thanks a lot El. I just need some time."

"Why don't you tell your old friend El what's going on?"

"I can't right now. Maybe when I get it sorted out."

"Well, you let us know if there is anything we can do. Suzy and I will be glad to help."

"I know El; you're both good friends. Thanks again. Good night."

"Good night."

Charity paced the room for some time. *I can't just show up on his doorstep and say, "Hi. I'm your long lost daughter, whom you never knew existed."* She continued to pace most of the night.

The next morning she contacted Alan Corey, her attorney. His secretary informed her that they had a slot open that morning, due to a cancellation.

"So what's going on?" Alan asked after they were both seated.

Charity explained the situation to him.

"Wow! That must have flabbergasted you!"

"To say the least."

"What do you want me to do, Charity?"

"I guess I thought that you would know how to break the news to him. Here's his address," she said as she handed it to him.

He was silent for awhile. "Well I could do some checking. I'm sure he has a lawyer or possibly a pastor. One of them might be able to help."

"Yes...maybe." She smiled for the first time since her mother had told her the truth about her father.

"There's something else you might not have

thought of."

"What's that?"

"Well, what if he doesn't believe that you're his daughter?"

"A blood test would prove that I am."

"True but you don't know what he's like. Maybe he won't want to know you."

"But...but." A feeling of dread started to sweep over her.

"I just want you to be prepared. You might be in store for some more heartache if he rejects you."

"Well that's a possibility."

He studied her before he spoke. "Okay Charity. I'll get right on it."

Besides the home that she shared with her mother, on their property there was an older, stone house of quaint European style that had been built by her great grandfather. He and his wife had been dairy farmers. In time her grandparents had taken over, but as the city started closing in around them, they had sold the cows and for ten years they raised chickens for the local markets. When her mother inherited the estate of nine acres she had sold all but two. Jean had moved in a factory built home for her and Charity to live in. The older house lacked the adequate wiring to support their electronic equipment. It was now used primarily for storage but two rooms had been set aside for guests.

Later the same day, she had talked to her lawyer; she hired a van to move her belongings to the older house.

When her mother came home she saw Charity's car parked at the old house. At first she didn't figure it out but after three hours went by, she checked Charity's room. Her eyes widened in disbelief, as she inhaled sharply and covered her mouth with her hand when she saw that it was empty. Jean hadn't really believed that Charity would move out. She ran to the window and looked at the other house. Evening shadows cast a mysterious obscurity on its surroundings but she could see that Charity's car was still there.

Chapter 2

"Dad," Clover Wayne, Steve's half-Blackfoot Indian daughter, called from the hallway.

"Yes," Steve answered from his den, not looking up from his paper work.

"Pastor Evan is here."

"Have him come in."

Clover opened the door wide enough for the pastor to go through. As the two men shook hands, Steve spoke. "I was surprised when you called. The last time you came out here on a non-social call was when my dear wife Sweet Flower died."

"Yes I know," he stated, when they were both seated.

"Could I get you something, coffee, tea or water?"

"No."

"Well, what's this all about?"

"Let's have prayer first."

"Okay."

The pastor prayed for wisdom and for Steve, that God would give him strength.

Steve could feel his heart beat speed up. "This must be serious," he said softly, after the pastor had finished the prayer.

"It is."

"Well, Evan, you and I have been through a lot together. You're the one who helped me get over the bitterness I felt when Jean left me. I blamed God, but in time I learned to lean on Him. If you hadn't been there for me, I probably would have turned into a sour, spiteful old man."

"Thanks for those kind words."

"So what have you got to tell me, Evan?"

"You're going to have to be prepared for a little shock."

. "Is it that bad?"

"No Steve. It's a good shock."

"What could be a good shock?"

"I guess I ought to start at the beginning. When Jean left you, she was pregnant."

Steve focused on his pastor, unable to speak as his mind assimilated Evan's words.

Evan told him about Charity.

He was stunned. He looked down at his desk then at last Steve spoke. "She's a veterinarian?"

"Yes. She and her partner have a practice in San Diego."

"She...she didn't know about me?"

"Not until three days ago."

"I'd say we both have had a shock."

"Yes. She's furious with her mother."

"That's understandable...How do you know she's my daughter? Don't we need to get blood tests?"

"Yes, you do. She's already got hers."

"I'll see if I can get mine this afternoon. We should know in a few days… then." He paused. "Let's keep this to ourselves until we get the results."

"Of course."

A week later Steve and Charity both knew that she was his daughter. Wearing jeans, boots, a sheepskin coat and a tan Stetson, Steve sat on the front porch and thought about what he had just learned. *I wonder if she's like her mother, tall and beautiful.* He felt joy and sadness all at the same time, joy that he had another daughter and sadness for all the years that they had missed.

None-the-less he was grateful for the good life he had experienced with Sweet Flower and Clover. Clover was a lot like her mother in physical ways but Sweet Flower had been soft and gentle, whereas Clover was headstrong and wild like her tough aboriginal grandfather.

Absentmindedly his eyes scanned the lane from the house to the country road, lined with rock fir and lodge-pole pine trees. Patches of lawn, still brown from winter, streaked with remnant snow, spread out on either side of the lane and connected with the horse and cattle pastures, separated by white rail fences. The pleasant odor of pine delicately perfumed the atmosphere. In the north pasture numerous Herefords moved about searching for the sparse bits of grass that weren't adequate to sustain them, so they were fed daily from the barns of stored hay until the pasture land would again yield its crop. On the south side, quarter horse geldings and pregnant mares foraged in the same way. Mooing, an occasional whinny and the twittering of brave, early, feathered friends were the only sounds to be heard in the crisp, midday air.

Evergreen bushes had been strategically planted in the flowerbeds, skirting the two-story white wood framed ranch house. In between the bushes, crocuses bloomed and an occasional tulip had pushed a green tip just above the ground, as if to

14

test the temperature before completely emerging.

He wasn't aware of Clover's presence until she took the chair next to him. "What's the mystery Daddy? You haven't been yourself for days."

Clover's sleek black straight hair hung halfway down her back. High cheekbones in a flawless olive complexion complemented her vivid blue eyes, which she had inherited from her father and could turn to steel when she got angry.

Steve reached over and took her hand. Then he told her about Charity.

She went ridged and said nothing.

"When you get over the trauma of this, I'm sure you will be glad to have a sister."

Clover was a master at hiding her feelings. "I'm sure you're right Daddy," she lied.

"Evan called and told me that Charity is going to phone me at one-o'clock." He checked his watch. It was five minutes to one. "Do you want to talk to her?"

"Not yet, Daddy."

"I understand."

They were both silent, each absorbed in their own thoughts.

When the phone rang, Clover rose and went into the house.

"Hello." Steve held his breath.

"Hello...are you Steve Wayne?"

"Yes... Charity?" His heart rate increased.

"Uh...yes. You're my dad."

"So it seems." He thought that he heard her sniffle. His eyes started to moist over.

"I...want to see you."

15

There was a pause. "Me too. We have a lot of catching up to do."

"Well...I'm glad that you want to meet me also. I...I already made reservations."

His heart pounded harder. "To fly out here?"

"Yes...If that's...okay."

"Of course." He could tell that she was crying softly.

"I'll stay in a motel."

"Absolutely not, you'll stay at the ranch!"

"Uh...are you sure? I...don't want to put you out."

"Put me out!... Oh daughter!...I want to spend as much time as I can with you."

"Uh....I'm...sorry...but...I." She was sobbing louder.

"I know, daughter, it's okay. You cry as much as you need to."

"Uh...I...just ...can't talk much...more."

"You need to know that you have a sister."

"Alan....my attorney, told...me."

"When does your plane arrive here?"

"One...pm...tomorrow." She managed to choke out the words.

"Okay. I'll have Clover pick you up."

"I... have... to go."

"Okay daughter. She'll have a sign with her. I'll see you tomorrow."

"Bye...Dad."

Steve sat on the porch long after he had talked to Charity. *Oh my God, what a revelation. I can hardly fathom it!*

He went to find Clover. She was sitting in the large country kitchen at the table, with a cup of coffee.

"Would you like some coffee, Dad?"

He shook his head. He told her about Charity's schedule.

"That's tomorrow."

"Yes, I won't be able to meet the plane. Doctor Ross is coming out to check the cows that have been aborting their calves. You will have to pick her up."

"Sure, Dad. How long is she staying?"

"Two weeks."

He didn't see the look of relief on her face.

Chapter 3

Charity hadn't spoken to her mother since the evening she had run out of the house. Several times Jean had tried to call her but when Charity saw that it was her mother's number she would shut her phone off. At last Jean swallowed her pride and went over to the old house and walked in. She didn't announce herself; instead she quietly went from room to room, until she spied Charity standing on the back porch.

"There you are," she stated as she stepped out.

Charity gazed at her, but didn't say anything.

"Uh...I was hoping we could talk."

Charity turned her back on her mother and fixed her eyes on the jade shading the house, which her grandmother had planted before Charity was born. "What about?"

"I want you to come home...I..."

"I am home, Mother."

"You know what I mean, move back where you belong."

She turned around and glared at her mother. "You know Mom; I'm not sure where I belong."

"I don't understand."

"Well maybe I belong in Montana."

"But...but this is your home. You have a practice here."

"I might just move, practice and all. People do that all the time."

"What! You can't mean it!"

"I'm seriously thinking about it."

"What put that notion into you're head?"

"It started developing when I talked to Dad on the phone."

"You'd better spend a little time in Montana, before you make a decision to move there. It's a hard country."

Charity again, turned her back on her mother. "I'm going to. I'm leaving tomorrow."

Jean walked over and stood by her daughter. "I mean you need to be there in the winter. You haven't any idea how cold it can get."

"Is that why you left him?"

"Partly."

"What else went wrong?"

Jean was silent for a moment. "I'm not going to run him down. I don't want you to have any preconceived ideas about him. It might cloud your first impression. We both made mistakes."

Charity turned and briefly scrutinized her mother. Her heart softened a little. "I will say you have changed. Before you started going to that church, you weren't so tolerant."

Jean didn't answer. She swallowed hard and changed the subject. "What about your practice here?"

"A semi-retired vet is going to fill in for me, for a couple of weeks."

"I see." Jean put her arm around her daughter's neck.

Charity didn't pull away, but she didn't return the affection either.

"Could I drive you to the airport?" Jean asked.

"Sure, if you want to."

"I want to."

"It's a good thing we started early. This traffic is awful," Charity stated, as they crept along at twenty mile an hour.

"I knew we would run into some road construction on Martin Luther King, so that's why I wanted to leave home a little early."

"I'm glad."

"It won't be much longer. I think the construction ends when we cross fifteenth."

Charity changed the subject. "Mom, you said that you loved Dad, so I don't understand why you left him."

Jean didn't answer for awhile then carefully chose her words. "I was too young, but I did try and might have stayed, if it hadn't been for that winter."

"What do you mean?"

"A Siberian front blew in and the winter from hell hit. The temperature went down to forty below zero, with a wind chill factor of about sixty below."

"So, you were in a warm house...Right?"

"Yes, but your dad was working non-stop, to try to save as many animals as he could and get hay to them. So I had to chop wood and haul it in, keep the fires going twenty-four hours a day. I made trips to the stores and pumped gas until my face was numb and I couldn't feel my hands. Then there were the chickens, goats and rabbits to tend, because every available hand was needed to help your dad."

At last they left the construction behind, as they crossed over highway fifteen.

Charity was silent for some time before she spoke again. "So what you're saying is that you just ran out on him. He must have come home to a cold

20

house." Her voice was sharp.

"Uh...yes I did run out on him, but he didn't come home to a cold house. I banked both fires, fixed a meal for him, took care of the animals and left him a note."

"What do you mean banked the fires?"

"The fire is allowed to burn down to coals then ashes are placed over the coals. The coals will burn slowly and won't go out."

"I would think that ashes would smother the coals and they would go out."

"If too many ashes are used, that can happen."

"It must have been difficult for him after you left." Her voice hadn't lost its sharpness.

"He hired an Indian woman right after I left to run the house. I think she was the one he eventually married."

"How did you know about that?"

"I had a friend, Millie, who kept me informed for awhile."

"What do you mean, for awhile?"

"We lost track of each other, due to time and distance."

Jean took the ramp to interstate five going north. Soon Charity could see San Diego Bay and North Island.

Neither spoke as they sped along, Jean concentrating on her driving and Charity thinking about her trip and meeting her dad and Clover.

When they arrived at the airport, Jean helped Charity with her luggage. She didn't try to hug or kiss her daughter instead she said goodbye and left to go to work.

Chapter 4

Clover took the sign that read, 'Welcome Charity', her father had made. She sneered as she looked at it. *I'll make her welcome, all right.* She walked towards the building. *I'm not going to let that 'witch of a white eyes,' hurt Daddy like her mother did. Besides I'm not going to share Daddy's love.*

She entered the building, just as the first of the passengers were coming down the concourse. An attractive young woman neared Clover. *I bet that tall Nordic type is her.* But to Clover's surprise, the woman glanced at the sign and kept on going, until she flew into the arms of a waiting cowboy. Then a cute blond, of average height, with warm brown eyes that were searching the waiting group of people approached Clover. When she saw the sign, a look of relief came over her face. Clover's heart sunk. She wasn't at all what she had expected. *I don't care if you are nice; I'm not going to like you, besides looks can be deceiving.*

Both girls looked each other up and down. "You're Clover." Charity said, with a smile.

"Not to you," she snapped. "Only people I like, call me that. You call me Gayle."

Charity was momentarily taken aback but unbeknown to Clover, Charity was tougher than she looked. She had fought her way through veterinary school. In spite of the politics, she had survived and it being a predominantly male field, she had met with much opposition. There was something about resistance that made Charity rise to the challenge. She smiled sweetly. "I have to pick up my luggage, *Gayle.*"

It was Clover's turn to be surprised. However having the ability to hide her feelings, she shrugged her shoulders and silently followed Charity to the baggage claim area. She took note of Charity's slim, jeans clad figure as Charity watched for her cases. *You're just a little city chick and I'm not going to help you with your luggage. I'll let you struggle on your own.* Then, Clover was even more surprised at Charity's strength, as she lifted the heaviest case with ease with her right hand and grabbed an overnight bag with her left. .

When they reached the ranch truck, Clover motioned for Charity to put her luggage in the back. *Now I bet you'll have trouble lifting that heavy one.* But to Clover's chagrin, Charity effortlessly raised the bag and placed it into the high truck bed. *Okay, so you're strong. I'll have some other tests for you that will be harder to pass.*

When Clover left the airport she headed east.

Charity kept looking all around as they drove. "Compared to the hustle and bustle of San Diego, this traffic moves at an easy pace. And the buildings aren't as tall. I've never been to any place like this before."

"So you think this is a hick town, huh?"

"No, not at all. I think it's cool and laid back."

"Yah, right."

Charity ignored her.

Fluffy white tuffs, like huge snowflakes were drifting through the air. Charity studied them as they fell on the truck and against the windshield and then were blown away, as the vehicle moved down the road.

"What's that?"

"Cotton from the cottonwood trees," Clover answered begrudgingly.

"It's kind of pretty."

"It's a nuisance and messy." She sneered.

As they moved away from the town, the houses were farther apart and Charity saw rolling pastures, graced with evergreen trees and dotted with foraging cattle, horses, goats, donkeys and mules.

Charity leaned over, looked up and out the window. "Amazing."

"What?"

"It's the sky. It's so clear, big and blue!"

Clover didn't respond. *You are a city ditz, all bright eyed and dull-witted.*

When they drove down the lane towards the house, Steve was sitting on the porch and Doctor Ross was just leaving. He waved at Clover as he backed his truck up, then turned and headed down the lane. Charity didn't bother to ask Clover who he was.

Steve stood up when the women stepped out of the truck. He and Charity gazed intently at each other and time stood still. Clover watched them. *It's going to be tougher than I thought, to drive a wedge between them.* Next he bound off of the porch, hugged Charity and swung her around. Subsequently they stood still, looked at each other for a moment, still embracing. No one spoke. Clover momentarily glanced away. Jealousy ate at her core. He pushed Charity back and studied her face. She was flushed and tears bathed her eyes.

"You're not at all what I expected." Steve found his voice.

"What did you expect?"

"A tall brunette."

"I hope you're not disappointed."

"No not at all. You're cute as a button."

"And you're tall and strong."

"That's what all the girls say."

They both laughed.

Clover started toward the house with her back to them. Steve grabbed Charity's suitcase. She took the smaller bag, then he put his other arm around her and they followed Clover into the house.

"We can talk and get acquainted, as soon as you're settled." He carried her bag up the stairs. Clover followed her father, with Charity behind her.

"Clover, show Charity her room," Steve stated and headed back down.

"Sure Dad."

After passing by one door she opened the next one. "This is it." she stated briskly.

"It's nice."

Clover watched her for awhile, as she started to unpack. "Dinner's at seven," she stated and left.

Later Steve showed Charity around, starting with the chickens. "Those white and gray ones are Plymouth Rocks. We raise them for our frequent chicken dinners. The all white chickens are Leghorns; they're better layers."

"Did you know that Mom's parents had a chicken

farm?"

"Yes I did." He smiled down at her. "By the way, how is Jean?"

"She's okay."

He steered her toward the corral. "Do you ride?"

"A little."

"You can pick out a horse to ride while you're here, if you like. Clover can help you. Some might be too spirited for you." Sharing the corral with five mares was a shiny, black stallion. "The black is my Tennessee walker," Steve volunteered.

"He's beautiful. What's his name?"

"Midnight."

A chestnut quarter horse with a white blaze ran over to the fence. "Well, aren't you a pretty one?" Charity stated.

"That's Dory. She's nosey, spirited and skittish."

"I like her." Dory stuck her head over the fence. Charity rubbed her nose.

"Well, I'll be. She's never let anyone else touch her nose."

"I'll have to bring her a carrot, the next time I visit her."

As she continued to rub Dory's nose, Charity's eyes scanned the terrain. "The mountains are so big and beautiful."

"The Indians called Montana the land of the shining mountains, mainly because the Belt Mountains, in the Bob Marshall Wilderness always have snow on them. Over there to the east are the Little Belt Mountains."

"Oh they're lovely! And they do shine with the snow on them, just like you said."

Clover watched Charity and Steve from a distance. An inferno bubbled inside her. Gus, one of Steve's ranch hands, sat perched on the fence near by.

"Ya air crusin toards trouble, Missy." He said, as he shrewdly studied her.

"What do you mean?" Her outward appearance was calm. However Gus knew her very well.

"Ya knows what old Gus means." He glanced back at Charity and Steve. "Put a bridle on hit, afore hit takes ahold of ya."

She loved Gus. He was like a second father to her. He was rough and gruff, as he was honest and loyal. What he lacked in, 'book larnin' to quote him, he had an uncanny ability to judge character, to perceive situations as they really were and usually acted wisely, accordingly. They had adopted him into their family a long time ago or maybe it was the other way around.

She pretended that it was a joke. "Now Gussy." She laughed. "Where did you come up with such an ominous idea?"

"I tole ya not ta call me Gussy...and cut out them fancy words." He turned sharp, squinty, hazel eyes on her. His face, deeply lined from years of tough outdoor living, was framed by graying hair that stuck out from beneath his battered old Stetson. "Now ya listen ta Gus. Don't ya start sompun that's apt ta bring yar dad a heap of pain and could bust up yar family."

"I really don't know what you mean." She turned on her heel and marched towards the house.

He watched her until she disappeared inside, then he shook his head and headed toward the stables.

When they sat down to eat, Steve asked the blessing.

Clover had prepared venison stew and biscuits. Both Steve and Charity gave her favorable complements.

"Would you like some help with the cooking?" Charity asked Clover.

"Oh no, you're a guest."

"I wouldn't mind...really. I could fix breakfast. One of my specialties is pineapple pancakes."

"Umm...that sounds good," Steve stated.

"I could make them in the morning, if you like."

"Do we have pineapple?" Steve asked Clover.

"Yes, canned chunks."

"Good, chunks work better in pancakes than the crushed. You don't mind if I make them tomorrow, do you Clover?"

"Not at all. I'll show you where everything is in the kitchen, later."

"By the way, Clover, Charity has taken a fancy to Dory. Do you think she would be okay for her to ride?"

Clover gave him a skeptical look. "I wouldn't recommend her. How well do you handle a horse, Charity?"

"Not too badly. I started riding when I was eight."

"Dory requires a strong hand. I think you should pick one of the more gentle mares, such as Alice. She's suitable for a city girl who's been riding easygoing mounts."

"I would like to try Dory, Dad."

"I don't know. Clover's fairly good at assessing when it comes to horses. I don't want you to get hurt."

"What if I ride her around the corral first? Then you can judge for yourself if I can handle her."

"Well...what do you think Clover?"

"Sure, but remember Charity, I warned you." *She'll dump you before you can count to ten.* Her expression was enigmatic.

Later Clover took Charity to the kitchen and opened the pantry.

"Here are the canned goods," she stated, as she took down a can of pineapple. "There's four more up here. There're fifteen ounces in each can. And over here is the pancake mix." She moved to another cupboard and placed a bag on the counter.

"Oh, I hope you have flour. I like to make the cakes from scratch."

"I have a little in here," she said in surprise. Clover opened up the largest of the white crock canisters. "I didn't know anyone made pancakes from scratch anymore."

"That's enough," Charity declared as she examined the contents.

"What else do you need?"

"Baking powder, shortening, salt, sugar, vanilla and the griddle."

"What's the sugar and vanilla for?"

"Syrup."

"You're full of surprises, aren't you, *sister?*"... Just remember to clean up afterwards. Your mother doesn't live here"

Charity smiled sweetly and didn't respond to the

barb, which infuriated Clover.

After Charity left the kitchen, Clover took a heaping tablespoon of salt, dumped it into the flour and stirred it around, smirking triumphantly. *That should make your pancakes memorable, sister dear.*

Later Clover stood gazing out the kitchen window. In the twilight, evening shadows swept across the back lawn and the corral. There Charity was petting Dory as she fed her a carrot. *Bribery won't help, sister dear. Dory is unpredictable. I'm going to enjoy watching you land on your nose.*

Chapter 5

Charity stretched, yawned and sat up on the edge of the bed. She switched on the bedside lamp. Her watch indicated that it was six am. She went across the room and opened the drapes. Charity caught her breath at the beauty of the sunrise, as a brilliant circle of light was slowing rising from behind the Little Belt Mountains. She watched it as it splashed burnished gold in striated streaks, intermittently with violet, in the cobalt sky. Slowly the gleaming sphere moved above the horizon and hung in a fiery starburst, edged by orchid. Gradually daylight started to take command of the land, as the colors began to fad away and the blue sky took their place. Three groves of lodge pole pine, miles apart shared the land with quaking aspen. Standing bleakly, the aspen's branches, dry and bare in the crisp air, were awaiting warmer weather to send out leaf buds.

March had arrived gently. Portions of snow sparkled like diamonds under the luminous rays of the sun. They rested in a patch work pattern, alternating with sprigs of tender grass, the beginning of new pasture that would soon be the livestock's main food source. A robin, with a twig in his beak, one of many early yearly visitors, lit momentarily on a corral post before resuming flight to where he was constructing a nest for the next generation. In the corral, Midnight looked in the direction of the house, shook his head and whinnied, then as he moved about, the other horses got out of his way, bowing to his domination.

Charity sighed and reluctantly left the window to lay out her clothes and take a shower.

Soon after, in the kitchen, she made the syrup first. When it was cooked she removed it from the stove and blended in the vanilla. Next she used the hand mixer to combine the ingredients for the batter, before she folded in the pineapple. When the griddle was hot she fried one small cake. It was always her habit to taste test her cooking. After taking a bite, she quickly spit it into the garbage. *Oh! Something's wrong with the flour.* Charity spooned some up and touched it with her tongue. *Aha...Clover you tried to set me up. Well, sister dear...I found you out.* Charity dumped most of the batter down the garbage disposal, took a clean bowl out of the cupboard, grabbed the pancake mix and another can of pineapple. In a few minutes she was frying another test cake. About then Steve walked into the kitchen.

"Good morning," he stated, as he kissed her on the cheek.

"Good morning Dad." She smiled up at him. "I'm glad you're up."

"I've been up for over two hours, Daughter." His vivid blues eyes twinkled as he smiled back at her. "Is breakfast about ready?"

"Yes. Do you want some eggs or bacon with these pancakes?"

"A couple of eggs, over easy."

"Okay. Is it all right if I fry them in some bacon drippings?"

"Sure." He paused. "I'm so glad that we found each other, Charity."

"Me too, Dad." She hugged him. "I better get busy," she said after an awkward moment.

"Well I'll let you alone." He sat down at the kitchen table with the morning paper.

She fried a couple of slices of bacon then placed the eggs on the griddle and when they were cooked, she took them to her father.

About then Clover came in and sat down at the table. She was careful not to be rude to Charity in front of her father. So she greeted her.

"Good morning." Charity responded. "Would you like some bacon and eggs?"

"One slice of bacon and one egg, over easy, please."

Charity fried the bacon and egg and then put on four pancakes to cook before she took Clover's breakfast to her.

Soon Steve sampled the first cake. Charity watched Clover's face. "Yum...very good," he expounded.

Clover reached over and broke off a piece of Steve's cake and popped it into her mouth. A stoic expression remained on her face.

"Hey! Get your own," Steve chided her, good-naturedly. His chiseled features were neatly capped by thick, graying, sandy hair.

"Would you like some pancakes, *sister*?" Charity asked, smiling sweetly.

"Yes, I would."

"It will only take a few minutes."

She took the rest of the salty batter and made two cakes for Clover. Presently she placed Clover's pancakes in front of her. Then she sat back to savor the show, as she watched Clover apply ample amounts of butter and syrup before taking a big bite of cake. Clover held the bite in her mouth for a split second then calmly chewed and swallowed it, laid her fork down and rose from her chair. She didn't look at Charity.

Steve stared at Clover. "What's the matter?"

"My eyes were bigger than my stomach. I'm full. I'll see you later."

Charity didn't say anything; she just grinned as she watched Clover leave the room.

"How odd," Steve stated.

Recess lighting, in the plaster ceiling, illuminated the pale yellow walls and oak cupboards in the large country kitchen. Three feet away an island cabinet held a counter top stove. A metal, circular rack hung from the ceiling directly overhead and sustained various copper bottomed, steel pots and pans. The Formica counter tops, appliances and doweled kitchen table and chairs were all off white. The furnishings stood in a three-sided alcove, at one end. A gold fixture with three prongs, each holding a lamp socket that was concealed by a fluted, milk glass shade, produced a soft light for the area. Bright yellow Pricilla curtains enhanced the windows, which took up at least one half of each wall. Charity smiled to herself as she cleaned up. *I'm leaving it shining and spotless.* After she loaded the dishwasher and wiped off the counters, she polished the faucets and handles on the sink. Then she swept and mopped the yellow, off white and gold flecked tile floor, but she didn't dump out the salty flour. *I hope you forget and use it for one of your culinary creations, sister dear.*

Later she meandered into the spacious living room. It was furnished with typical ranch style furniture. Two large couches and two oversized chairs, upholstered in brown and white cowhide, shared the room with rustic pine tables and sidepieces. A large brown leather recliner, in spite of its modern design, blended well with the rest of the furniture. A green, yellow and gold braided oval rug covered most of the shiny wooden floor. Only a few pictures hung on the walls and they were country scenes. A massive stone fireplace dominated one wall. To one side was a built in entertainment center and on the other side were shelves supporting books and pictures. Down a hallway, Steve's office was next to the master bedroom. She could hear male voices coming from behind the closed door.

About then a plump, plain, forty some lady in sweats walked through the front door. "Hello," she said when she saw Charity, "I'm Molly, Steve's housekeeper."

"Charity Wayne, Steve's daughter."

The housekeeper was stunned and speechless.

"I know. It's a shock. Neither Steve, my dad, nor I, knew that the other one existed until about a week ago."

"My...my," Molly exclaimed, when she found her voice. She removed her glasses and pushed strands of errant, mousy brown hair into a bun on the back of her head. "You and Clover aren't anything alike."

"That's true. Probably because we had different

mothers."

"Hum...yes...Clover's mother was Sweet Flower." She produced a tissue from her handbag and wiped her glasses, before she placed them back on her face.

"Did you know her?'

"Yes, indeed. For several years. She was the mistress of this house. But it was Mister Steve who always gave the orders. She was meek and unassuming."

"Did you know my mother?"

"Do you mean Jean?"

"Yes."

"I knew of her but I never met her. Some say that she was a real beauty but not suited to hard ranch life."

"I'm not like my mother. She's tall and a brunette."

"Well I have to get busy," Molly said after a pause. "I'm pleased to meet you, Charity."

"Same here." She watched Molly walk, in black oxfords, toward the back of the house.

Then Charity found a woman's magazine addressed to Clover and sat down to scan it. An article about raising hybrid roses caught her eye. She hadn't finished with it when Steve's door opened. A tall, well built, darkly handsome man paused when he saw her before he moved down the hall and into the room. Steve was right behind him.

"Charity," Steve stated. "This is my foreman, Billy Blake. Billy, meet my daughter, Charity."

Momentarily Billy looked astounded then he smiled, displaying pearly white teeth. "I can see that you're surprised." Steve told him briefly how he and Charity found each other.

Billy looked even more amazed.

"Actually it's a long story, Billy." Steve changed the subject. "We'll talk more later about the cows that have been aborting."

"Okay, boss." Billy flashed Charity another toothy smile. "It was a pleasure meeting you, Charity."

You're a charmer but I'm not sure if I trust you. Charity didn't answer him instead she nodded.

"You don't like him." Steve stated, after Billy left.

"I'm not sure. He seems kind of slick to me."

"Well, he's sort of a ladies man, but when it comes to ranching, he knows his business. His father John Blake owned one of the biggest spreads around here. Billy grew up learning all about it. Sadly, the ranch would be Billy's today, if his father hadn't lost it gambling."

"He looks Native American."

"Yes, he's one half, like Clover. His mother was a Black-foot maiden. His grandfather, Charley Hawk Claw and Billy's sister Bonnie live on a farm, up on the west side of King's Hill Pass."

"Interesting."

Yes, Billy has hunted and ridden all over this part of the country. He knows every inch of it, from the Helena National Forest, east of highway 15, west to Broadwater county, north to the Gates of the Montana Wilderness and as far south as Jefferson County."

"Dad, I heard you say something about some of your cows aborting their calves."

"I don't want to burden you with it, Charity."

"I know Dad but I am a veterinarian. Maybe I can help."

"Well okay. Let's get a cup of coffee and I'll tell you all about it."

Later they were both sitting at the kitchen table. "It started about three weeks before you came. We lost about half of the calves."

"That's awful. What did your vet say?"

"Norman Ross came out then and said it was probably brucellosis, commonly known as Bang's disease, so we isolated those cows from the rest of the herd. We were careful to dispose of the fetuses and the afterbirths and clean up the areas"

"But when you were talking to Billy, it sounded like you've had more of the cows aborting."

"Yes after we isolated the first ones, I thought it was under control, but a few days before you came here, five more cows lost their calves."

"What kind of tests did your vet do?"

"He drew blood but the tests came back negative. Of course the tests are inconclusive as they could have the disease and it hasn't shown up in the tests yet."

"If it is brucellosis, your cattle could have contacted it from bison."

"True but there hasn't been any bison on my range for several years."

"What about new stock...or a new bull."

"No."

"I can't practice in Montana, but I can do some research. Maybe Norman has overlooked something."

"Like what?"

"Well one thing can imitate something else."

"What do you mean?"

"Awhile back at the clinic, a lady brought in a female collie named Suzy that started vomiting every morning. We thought it was her diet because the lady let Suzy eat whatever she was eating. People food isn't good for dogs, especially things like ice cream and donuts. She stopped feeding her anything but dog food and Suzy continued to vomit."

"Was she pregnant?"

"Yes, but we had ruled that out, because the owner had assured us that Suzy hadn't been with a male."

"Well some stud got to her."

"Yes, you see she had a large back yard for Suzy to run in and the next door neighbor had a German shepherd. Come to find out the shepherd would jump the fence. No one had seen them together, but one day Suzy's owner happened to look out and saw the shepherd jump back into his own yard. You can imagine how upset she was when Suzy dropped, what her owner called, four little half-breeds. Soon after that she had the top of the fence extended, which ended any future romantic pursuits of the shepherd."

"Well I am concerned because I'm losing money. I would like to get this straightened out as soon as possible. If it keeps up, I could lose the ranch."

"Oh Dad!"

He covered her hand with his. "Now don't you worry about this. It's in God's hands. Besides this ranch and I have weathered some real tough times through the years."

"Okay Dad, but I'm going to see what I can find out, just the same. You know there are some plants that the cows could have ingested that would cause them to abort."

"True, but why all of a sudden? Surely the plants would have been out there on the range all the time. Why now?"

"The seeds could have blown in or came in on a wild animal's coat such as a coyote, wolf or other wild animal. Another mode of transportation could be on someone's clothing. Then when the plants grew, they were harvested in the hay. I'd like to check out the pasture; where you keep your breed cows and the hay barn."

"Okay, we can see them from the back porch."

She rose and followed him.

"See off to the east is that pasture and if you look just to the right you can see the hay barn."

Later Charity and Steve spent the evening looking through his albums. He showed her pictures of her grandparents and other relatives, mostly deceased. Then he turned to a picture of Jean and him. The handsome young couple, in western attire, had happy expressions on their faces. Charity gazed at it for some time. A feeling of sadness came over her.

"We were on our way to the fair and rodeo. My mother, your grandmother took that picture."

"I'm surprised you kept it, Dad."

"Why not, Charity? After all we were married."

"Oh I don't know...I would think you'd want to forget about what happened then."

"Charity, your mother was a part of my life. Besides you're here now and you're a constant reminder that she and I were together."

The next day Charity went to the library and checked out some books on herbal medicine and an herbal Physicians' Desk Reference. After several hours of pouring over the herbal medicine books she came up with one or two that could cause miscarriages in humans but only one, which could be grown locally. Going to the Physicians Desk Reference, she found out that the root either fresh or dried was used in some cultures to relieve menopausal symptoms and some other types of female problems and could cause miscarriages in pregnant women. *Hmm... ground up, it could be mixed into hay and ingested.* The next step was to check the hay supply. *If it's in the hay, someone is sabotaging Dad.* Charity took a plastic food bag from the kitchen and waited until no one was around, to investigate the hay barn. Fortunately there was a bale that had been broken open. Looking closely, she found small chunks of a substance other than hay. She took sufficient samples and ran them into the agricultural lab.

"I'm not authorized to do this, ma'am," the young laboratory technician stated.

"Couldn't you make an exception? Please." She told him what she suspected.

He whistled through his teeth. "I don't know. I could get into trouble but if you're right, something needs to be done." He scratched his head. "I know and respect your dad and I wouldn't want anyone to get away with such a thing." He paused for a moment. "Okay, leave the bag here. Come back in an hour."

She wandered through some shops, then found a cafe and got a soda.

When she went back to the lab, the technician met her at the door. "Holy cow, lady, you were right! There was enough of that herb in what you brought in here to make an elephant miscarry!"

"I sure appreciate you bending the rules a little. By the way my name is Charity."

They shook hands. "I'm Bobbie Carson. I'm glad I bent the rules, this time."

She hurried back to the ranch to show the report to her Dad. To her frustration he wasn't in the house. Clover was in the kitchen getting supper started. "Where's Dad," Charity asked.

"He went over to the Jordan ranch to talk with Josh. He'll be home in time for supper."

"Could you use a little help?"

Clover turned and glared at Charity. "No *sister*. I'm capable of making a meal."

Charity didn't answer instead she raised her eyebrows and looked sideways at Clover and left.

She waited until after they had eaten, then she asked her dad if they could talk in his office. She ignored the scowl on Clovers face, which Steve didn't see.

Steve looked at the report. "What does this mean and what is black cohosh?"

"It means that someone has been deliberately feeding those cows an herb called black cohosh, also known as squaw root, black snake root, rattle root, and rattle weed. It affects the hormones in the cattle, so they abort their calves."

Steve looked intently at her for some time. "Good Grief," he expounded, at last. "I hope it's not in all the hay."

"No, I don't think whoever is doing this could have enough of it for all your hay. Maybe all you have to do is destroy what's in that hay barn."

"I think you're right. I've got plenty of hay in the other barns and there will be enough grass soon, so they won't need the hay"

"Sadly one or more of your hands is trying to ruin you."

Steve slowly shook his head. "Most of them have been with me for years." He was silent for a moment. "I'll tell them that I know about it. Hopefully whoever is responsible will be afraid to do it in the future."

"Maybe not with the herb but I think they might try something else. Do you think you should call the sheriff?"

"For the time being, I want to keep him out of this. He's not a very good sheriff. I'm going to ask our neighbor Josh Jordan to run for the office. Elections are this coming November...But I'm getting off the subject... I can't tell you how grateful I am that you figured this out. However I'm not ruling out the possibility that some of my cows might have brucellosis. Not until we have conclusive blood tests."

"Of course."

Presently all the hands were told about the contaminated hay and it was removed from the barn and burned.

Afterwards two riders dismounted in a copse of pine trees. "You were careless. Now Wayne knows someone is sabotaging him," one man stated.

"How was I to know that girl would discover the cohosh?"

"It was stupid of you to leave that bale lying around open. You made it easy for anyone who might get suspicious."

"Don't worry. I have another plan."

"You better hold off for awhile."

"I will."

"Just remember. If you get caught, I don't know anything about this. And if you did implicate me, I would deny it and no one would take your word against mine."

"When this is over, you better keep your promise about my share of the land."

"Don't worry, I will. With my ranch and Wayne's together, I'll have the biggest spread in the west. I can afford to be generous."

Chapter 6

The next Saturday Steve invited Josh and Cal Jordan over for dinner. The brothers' spread joined Steve's on the south side. Their ranch was smaller but still impressive. Needless to say, they were both surprised when they met Charity, as the word hadn't gotten around yet about Steve's other daughter.

The dining room carried the same country design as the rest of the house, from the massive oak table and chairs, to the pale yellow and white striped wallpaper and the shiny, wood planked floor. A pewter chafing dish rested on an oak buffet at one end of the room, balanced at the other end by an antique pie closet. Copper inserts with decorative eyelet-like openings, ventilated the doors.

Clover had prepared a Caesar salad, veal roast, mashed potatoes, thick brown gravy and corn on the cob. She had reluctantly allowed Charity to make two banana cream pies. Charity noticed that the salty flour had been disposed of, as the canister was full. But just to make sure she tasted it when Clover wasn't looking.

Charity noted that neither of the brothers was handsome in the conventional way. Their features were too big and their hair was brown, thick and wiry. However they both were large in stature; had excellent physiques and a rugged charm that was attractive. Cal was talkative, but Josh seemed to be the strong silent type. His eyes were dark brown and intense. She chided herself for being fascinated by him. *I don't know if it's his aura of mystery or the way he looks at me...like he could read my mind...Whatever it is, I'm not letting my guard down.*

"I don't mean to pry but it must have been a shock for both of you to find out that you had another daughter, Steve, and you Charity, to learn that your father was alive after years of thinking that he died when you were very young," Cal stated, looking at Steve and then at Charity.

"Yes it was staggering for both of us and emotional as well." Steve stated.

"I can't describe the emotions I experienced at the time and I am still experiencing," Charity exclaimed.

Steve told them that Charity lived in San Diego. Cal looked surprised when Steve told them that she was a veterinarian, but Josh's expression was unreadable.

Steve changed the subject. "I need to tell you that there's a possibility that my herd could be infected with Bangs disease. However the blood tests have come back negative. We have taken all the needed precautions to keep it isolated."

Josh and Cal looked up from their plates. Cal whistled through his teeth, "Dang!" he said at last.

Josh studied Steve before responding. "I'm sorry to hear that. We haven't had any symptoms in our herd," he said in a gravelly voice.

"Let's pray that you don't." Steve didn't mention the black cohosh.

"I'll call you if we spot any signs," Josh stated.

They were all silent as they finished the main course.

"That was a fine meal, Clover," Cal stated.

Josh nodded. "Yes, very good."

"Thank you. Uh...Charity would you help me with the pies? "

"Surely."

They all wanted coffee so both girls disappeared into the kitchen.

"Back off, *sister dear.*" Clover whispered forcibly. Her eyes were piercing into Charity's.

"What are you talking about?" Charity asked out loud.

"Hush!" Clover whispered and put her finger to her lips.

"What's the big secret?" she whispered.

"Cut the act, *sister.*"

Charity shrugged her shoulders. "You're being ridiculous." She started to move away.

Clover grabbed her arm. "You know what I'm talking about."

"No I don't." She took a hold of Clover's hand and flung it away from her.

"Oh come on. We both know that you couldn't keep your eyes off of Josh."

Charity was momentarily speechless as she fixed her gaze on Clover. *I didn't know it showed.*

"Stop the innocent act. Josh and Cal are country boys. Neither one is wise to the wiles of a city girl like you. Beside you're going home soon, so leave Josh alone!"

"What do you care?" She asked flippantly, as she took a knife and started to cut a pie.

"Cal and Josh are my friends. We grew up together." Clover started to work on the other pie.

"You know it isn't any of your business...so you

back off, *sister dear.*"

Clover glared at her, opened her mouth to retaliate and then snapped it shut. She had obviously changed her mind. They worked in strained silence, dishing up and serving the dessert.

Later they all retired to the living room. Steve talked to Josh about running for sheriff.

"I've thought about it," Josh stated after a pause. "Cal is capable of managing the ranch...What do you think, Cal?"

"I think you should, Josh. You'd be great, especially since you minored in law enforcement in college."

Charity listened silently to the conversation and tried not to look at Josh. *I have to admit I am glad that Clover made me aware, that I was staring at Josh. I've never met anyone like him before...he's like someone out of a western movie...strong and self contained, capable of dealing with any problem.*

Later before Charity got ready for bed she stood looking out her bedroom window. The moon was full and she could see the corral that held the horses. She watched Dory move around before settling in one spot for the night. Then to her surprise she caught sight of Clover as she walked away from the house. A man stepped out of the shadow of a pine tree and Clover moved into his arms. The man was Billy Blake. Charity dropped the shade and walked away from the window. *I feel like I'm spying.*

The next morning Steve convinced her to go to

48

church with him.

"What about Clover?"

Steve looked sad. "She hasn't gone for some time. She usually sleeps in on Sunday."

The only times Charity had been to church in her whole life had been for weddings and funerals. She listened to the pastor talk about something that she had never heard before. The title of the sermon was 'Jesus Died for You.' She carefully read each scripture, as he presented it to the congregation. *Hmmm...what he says is right out of the Bible.* Charity pondered what she had learned for the rest of the week.

Chapter 7

The next day Charity took in the beauty of the snow capped Garnet range to the west and the Little Belt Mountains on the east, glistening in the rays the morning sun as she approached the corral. The house blocked the Big Belt Mountains to the south. The valley between supported some of the largest ranches in the west, strategically located near the Missouri River.

She caught sight of an eagle soaring through the sky. Charity held her breath. *How extraordinary! He must have a wingspan of at least eight feet!*

Not a blade of grass stirred or a tree branch moved in the sunny crisp morning. The faint odor of pine, from scattered thickets of juniper bushes, was refreshing as Charity stood near the corral, stroking Dory's head.

"We're going to become good friends, Dory," she assured her as she opened her hand where a cube of sugar rested on the palm. Dory quickly gobbled up the morsel, then moved her head up and down and whinnied softly. Charity climbed over the rail and talking gently to her, she placed a bridle on Dory. Slowly she led the horse around the corral, stopping at intervals to stroke her and give her more sugar cubes. All the time she talked softly to her. Dory followed meekly. After about an hour Charity removed the bridle. "We'll do this again tomorrow, girl."

Four days in a row Charity repeated the same exercise with Dory. On the fifth day she put a saddle on her. At first Charity thought that Dory was going to buck. Instead she tried a few times to shake the saddle off, but Charity kept talking to her, gave her a carrot and soon Dory accepted the saddle. That evening Charity announced at the dinner table that she was going to try to ride Dory the next morning.

"Are you sure?" Steve asked.

"I'm sure."

Clover didn't speak. The smirk on her face said it all.

The following morning the other horses had been moved to the stables. Only Dory was waiting there when Charity arrived. Steve, Clover and Gus watched as Charity placed the bridle on Dory. Before Charity saddled her, she gave her a sugar cube and continued to talk softly to her. Dory didn't respond when Charity slipped on the saddle. Charity walked her around the corral once then painstaking she climbed into the saddle. Dory turned her head and eyed Charity before starting to crow walk. Charity was experienced enough to hold on tightly. All of a sudden Dory stopped and promptly lowered her head in an effort to dump Charity on the ground, but Charity had expected Dory to try to dismount her that way and tightened her thighs. After she straightened up, Dory took a few steps and reared up on her hind legs and pawed the air with her front legs. Again Charity held on. When that didn't work to dislodge her rider, she shied to the left and then to the right. But Charity remained in the saddle. Repeatedly Dory tried each maneuver. Finally Dory reared up on her hind legs again, by this time

Charity was exhausted. As though Dory sensed Charity's fatigue, she remained on her hind legs longer then before. It felt like an eternity to Charity. Just when she thought she couldn't hold on any longer, Dory came down on all four feet and stood still. Charity poked her lightly with her heels and urged her forward. Slowly Dory walked around the corral. Charity pulled on the reins and Dory stopped. Charity dismounted and led Dory around the corral one time then she climbed into the saddle again. This time Dory moved forward when Charity urged her with her heels and stopped when she pulled on the reins. Then Charity dismounted and came over to where the others were.

Gus and Steve clapped their hands. "Well you did it, Charity!" Steve expounded.

Gus smiled at Charity. "Ya air a fine little rider."

Clover didn't say a word. She turned around and marched into the house.

Steve watched as Clover slammed the door behind her. "Now what's the matter with her?"

Sour grapes, Daddy. "She didn't think I could ride Dory."

"But that was a strange reaction."

Not if you knew how she feels about me, Daddy.

The next day she decided to ride Dory outside the corral. She didn't take her more than a quarter of a mile down the lane and back. She knew it would be best to start out with short rides and gradually lengthen them. *Tomorrow I'll ride her to the east hay barn and back.*

That evening, when they had finished their supper, Billy came to talk to Steve. "I'm sorry to disrupt your evening, boss," he stated removing his hat and flashing Clover and Charity, each a captivating smile.

"That's okay, Billy. What's happening?"

"Harry and John found some deer hides, entrails and hooves on the east range, this morning. They had to be fresh as the coyotes hadn't gotten to them yet."

"Looks like we've got poachers again."

"Want me to take a couple of the hands and check it out?"

"No, likely they'll quit for a while. They were probably watching the boys, when they found the evidence."

"Are you sure?"

"Yaw, let's wait and see what happens...However I don't like it when strangers carry guns onto my land. It puts my men and animals at risk. A stray bullet could do a lot of damage."

"You're right. Okay, boss."

"While you're here, Billy, I'd like to talk to you about something else. Come on into the office."

Billy turned and smiled widely at Clover and Charity, again. "See you later, ladies," he stated, before following Steve through the door.

Clover stood and started clearing the table. Charity silently helped her.

"Sit down Billy," Steve stated, after Billy closed the door and Steve took the chair behind his desk. "I haven't had a chance to talk to you about the contaminated hay and that one or more persons are trying to ruin me."

"Yaw, when we were burning the hay, I wondered

53

who would want to do a thing like that."

"Somebody wants my land. They'll strike again, I'm sure."

"What do you want me to do, boss?"

"Unfortunately at least one of the men on this ranch is involved. I want you to keep your eyes open for me. You're out there with them. If anyone acts suspicious or you see anything unusual, I want you to report to me as soon as you can."

"Right boss, you can count on me."

As the day of her departure drew near a feeling of sadness crept into Charity's heart. She was going to miss the crisp, clean, fresh air, Dory and the slower easy pace, but most of all she would miss her father. Tears were close to the surface more than once when she thought about going back to San Diego. The day before she was to leave she rode Dory about five miles.

The following day her bags were packed and waiting at the foot of the stairs. She took one last trip to the corral. Dory whinnied and trotted over to the railing to meet her.

"Oh Dory, I'm going to think about you every day." Dory nosed her arm so Charity would stroke her. Then Charity gave Dory her fourth carrot of the day. "You're my friend." Charity kissed Dory above her nose, then turned and walked away. Dory whinnied again as though she understood what Charity had said.

She went into the house and to the kitchen where Clover was busy making a pie. "I came to say goodbye."

Clover looked up from her work, "Goodbye Charity." She didn't smile but she was pleasant.

Soon she and Steve were on their way to the airport "I know that you and Clover didn't get along very well," Steve stated, as he drove down the country road.

"I'm sorry, Dad."

"I don't think it was your fault. Clover is use to being the only one in my life. She can be a little possessive."

I think that's an understatement! "I'll call you often." She changed the subject, not liking the way the conversation was going.

He glanced in her direction. "I'll call you too, daughter."

After she confirmed her flight and checked her baggage, she had a fifteen-minute wait.

"I hope you will come back and visit, anytime. Your home is here, if you want it."

She almost told him that she was considering moving her practice to Montana, but she knew if she decided not to, it would hurt him. When it was time to board, she held back her tears. She hugged and kissed him, then turned and didn't look back. When she found her seat that was by the window she searched inside the terminal. When she saw him she waited to catch his eye and when she did, they waved to each other.

Soon the plane moved toward the runway and then sped forward for takeoff. She looked down as it soared through the clouds and left western Montana behind.

When Clover took the pie out of the oven to cool she put on her jacket and headed toward the corral. Dory watched her from the other side. "Come see what I have, Dory." Clover held up a carrot. Slowly hesitating suspiciously, Dory moved toward the treat. When she got almost within reach, she backed away whinnied and ran to the other side of the corral. Repeatedly Clover patiently coaxed her but each time Dory would almost take the carrot then run away. At last Clover gave up in disgust. She had no way of knowing that Dory was full of carrots.

Two weeks later, Doc Ross informed Steve that his herd was not infected with brucellosis.

Chapter 8

For several days after Charity returned to San Diego, she contemplated moving to Montana. She weighed the benefits and the disadvantages over and over in her mind. Charity had some friends that she had gone to school with and a few she had acquired in her profession, not to mention her partner, Elrod Lake and his wife. She was close to them. They treated her like a daughter. She would miss them all if she moved to Montana.

When she was ten she had gotten attached to a stray cat, she had named Rusty because he had long reddish brown hair. Later he had been so badly injured when he was hit by a car that eventually he had to be put down. She was impressed with the kindly doctor who had done his best to save him and had been compassionate, gently administering medication to relieve his pain. After that her passion was the care of injured and hurting animals. All her energy went into the cause, often helping friends with their pets. Sometimes a veterinarian would let her visit his clinic. When she was in high school she met Doctor Elrod Lake. Doctor Lake gave her a job after school and on Saturdays. He was touched by her zeal and encouraged her to go to veterinary school. She continued to work for him while she was getting her degree. She owed him a great deal. He would have to find someone else to take her place. She knew he would buy out her half of the partnership but she felt an obligation to him. Her heart was pulled in two directions.

Boyfriends had come and gone. She had never

been serious about any of them.

She missed her dad, Dory and the wide-open spaces. Finally she decided to contact the Montana State Board of Veterinary Medicine and check out the necessary requirements for getting licensed in that state. *Maybe looking them over will help me make my mind up. Besides if I do go to Montana to live, I can always fly back to San Diego for a visit. It's not like I'd be going to another planet, for heaven sake!*

She knew she should talk it over with her mother but she was still angry with her. And the hurt was deep. She didn't know if she would ever heal inside. When she was around Jean, she hurt the most, so she avoided her as much as she could. She continued to live in the old house. Jean was smart enough to give Charity her space.

At last she knew that she was going to live in Montana. She received her Montana license in the mail. It was hard to tell Elrod but when she did, he wasn't surprised.

"I could see it coming. I knew you had changed," he said sadly.

"But...I didn't say anything. How could you tell?"

"Charity, how long has it been? It has got to be more than ten years, since you came here with your special brand of compassion. I know you about as well as anyone does. From the time that you found out about your father, you have been discontent."

"Oh El, I'm sorry. You've been good to me."

"Now you listen to me. You earned my respect and my trust. You don't owe me a thing."

"But...but..."

"But nothing...think of it this way... if you had a special teacher and most of us have at one time or another...and...uh suppose he inspired you and made you want to do something unique with your life, would you feel obligated to stay in the same grade after you had passed the class just so you could pay homage to him?"

"But that's not the same. You gave me a job and taught me a lot."

"Charity, you worked for me...I paid you. You could have gotten a job frying burgers."

"But you patiently took time to teach me."

"So would a special teacher."

She hesitated. "But you're a good friend too."

"So... wouldn't you consider a special teacher one also?"

She chuckled.

"What's funny?"

"Well I'm beginning to think that you want to get rid of me."

"Now you know better than that."

She hugged him. "Yes I do El. I was only teasing."

Charity didn't tell anyone else about her decision until El had found a replacement for her. Then with trepidation she carefully planned to tell her mother. Charity asked her out to dinner at one of their favorite eating establishments. She waited until they had finished and talked her into an after dinner cup of coffee.

"Okay, Charity, I know that you have something to tell me."

She stared at her mother incredulously.

"Now my dear, you have been avoiding me, like I

had a contagious disease, then you call me out of the blue and ask me to have dinner with you...really Charity, I'm not brilliant but I'm not stupid either."

"Well...I...uh..."

"Let me make it easy for you. You're moving to Montana...Right?"

"Uh...Yes. How did you know?"

"Charity what else could it be...huh?"

"I must say, you are taking this very well."

"I've had plenty of time to think about it."

"Mom...I..."

"I know, dear. I pray that in time you will heal inside and we can be close again," she said sadly.

"I...I...don't know what to say."

"I understand."

The next day she called her dad and told him the news. He was ecstatic. "You can live at the ranch! That way we'll be able to see a lot of each other."

"I don't know yet" She was thinking about Clover, among other things. "We can figure that all out when I get there. I'm going to be busy setting up my clinic, so it might be better if I stay in town for a while."

He was silent for a minute. "Well, you're going to be here and that's what counts... By the way old Doc Ross has been threatening to retire for years. If you made him an offer on his clinic, he might take you up on it."

"Really!"

"Yes and you would have the advantage of an established clientele."

"I'll have my attorney look into it for me."

Chapter 9

The government had opened the gates to the higher elevations. The herds were driven up to the new grass. Ranchers had turned their breed bulls in with the cows, so that they would calve in February or March the following year.

The big sky country was buzzing with new life as the couple rode in silence. A fin-tail grouse darted across in front of Clover's buckskin, Ginger and Billy's black, White Socks, named for obvious reasons. They trotted along at a pleasant pace. Finally they slowed down, dismounted and sat down on a log that overlooked the clear, blue Missouri River. The rushing sound of it didn't drown out the pristine chorus. A crow scolded them for the intrusion, while a morning dove cooed and flitted from tree to tree. A meadowlark sang melodiously. Momma sparrows, blue birds and cedar waxwings were busy feeding their fledglings. The aroma of pine drifted in on a gentle breeze. Clover took in a deep breath and looked around taking in the splendor. It was one of those glorious May mornings. Cottonwood trees grew prolifically on either sides of the bank. Giant sunflowers gracefully bobbed on the air current, roaster heads, daisies and shooting stars decorated the countryside. The baby blue sky seemed to almost touch the ground, through the trees. She gazed up at the heavens. Only a few fleecy white clouds drifted overhead.

It had been a favorite place for them, since they were kids. They had been pirates, or Robin Hood and Maid Marian, or they had played hide and seek for hours.

"So the white princess is coming back to live here?" Billy asked with a sneer on his face.

Clover looked down at the ground. "Yes, she's going to stay at the house for now."

"I don't think she'll make it through the winter, especially if we have one of those killers, that Montana is famous for."

Clover turned her head and glanced at him. "I don't know Billy. She's tougher than you think."

"But she's a pampered city girl. I can't imagine her going out to tend a sick animal in forty degrees below zero temperatures, on icy roads, sometimes knee deep in snow."

"You might be right but what I've seen of her, she's strong, smart and tenacious."

Billy frowned. "I thought you didn't like her."

"I don't but I respect her in some ways." *Like one snake respects another.*

"Well I heard somewhere, that there was a code, among our Native American ancestors, that if a person could gain their respect, it was better than acquiring their love."

She giggled. "You've watched too many western movies."

"Just the same I'm going to ask grandfather about that the next time I see him."

"How is he and your sister?"

"They are both okay but he is getting old. I have tried to get him and Bonnie to come out of the wilderness. I would get them a little place in town."

"How old is he?"

"About eighty-five, I think."

He put his arm around her waist. For some time they sat silently enjoying the unspoiled surroundings, taking it all in. At last he kissed her, slowly and sweetly. Then gazing into her eyes he said, "I love you, Clover."

"Billy, I want to tell Dad about us," she stated breathlessly.

"I know sweetheart but the time isn't right."

"When will it be right Billy?"

"I'm not sure."

"Oh, Billy," she stated with annoyance and stood up.

"Be patient, my love." He stood up and pulled into his arms. "It won't be long."

"You promise."

"Yes I promise."

Chapter 10

I didn't take old Doc Ross long to make up his
mind to sell his practice and clinic to Charity. He
soon had visions of spending his days fishing and
hanging out with his cronies, most of whom had
already retired.

When Charity returned to Montana, Steve met her
at the airport and they went directly to the clinic.
Steve waited for her, as she looked the clinic over,
taking note of some improvements and changes she
would make. When Doc Ross got a break, he told
her that he could stay until she was ready to start so
she would have a chance to rest up from he trip. He
even offered to help her out at the clinic from time
to time, if she needed him and be on call for her
some weekends. They were able to settle on an
agreeable fee for his services.

The transfer took place two weeks later. His two
assistances, Joe Brown and Julie Harris both
decided to stay. Julie ran the office and sometimes
helped out with the animals. Joe would assist her
with the animals and also accompany her out into
the field, when she needed him.

After she moved to the ranch, she tried to stay out
of Clover's way and for a time all went well.

The time came to brand the calves. As Steve had
lost more than half of them, that season because of
the contaminated hay, it only took a couple of days.
Charity was glad that they finished up on Saturday
so she could watch.

Two large fire pits were burning, heating the irons
and keeping them hot. Men from the neighboring

ranches had come to help. Charity spotted Josh and Cal at one pit and Billy and Gus at another. Several men were working at each pit.

Steve had her stand by one of them and explained the procedure to her. "One by one Lou and Nat here will hold a calf down and Curt will burn the lazy *W* into its hide." She watched as Lou and Nat positioned an animal. It started to bawl. Then Curt held the Iron against the calf's hindquarter, for about ten seconds. She could hear it sizzle and she could smell the burning hair. After Curt placed the iron back in the pit he grabbed a knife and castrated the animal, dropping his testicles in a bucket. Most of the male calves were made steers. Five were set aside for future breeding animals.

Later she walked over to the other pit and observed, being careful to stay out of the way of the working men.

When lunchtime came, Clover arrived in a jeep pulling a small wagon that Steve helped her open up. Soon everyone was eating fried chicken, baked beans and biscuits served with hot coffee. All the utensils were paper, so each man, when he was finished eating threw his plate, fork and cup into the nearest fire pit.

That evening Charity got a call from her mother. The conversation was the usual niceties that casual friends might employ, both avoiding anything that could be painful. Charity patiently listened to her mother as she went on about her job and her church, sensing that Jean needed an excuse to keep her on the phone as long as she could.

One day, she had just left the bank and was on her

way back to the clinic, when she met Josh, coming down the street. As usual when she saw him an uneasy feeling crept into the pit of her stomach. *Why does that happen?* When he reached her he smiled slowly. She tried to smile back but her face muscles seemed to have a mind of their own and all she could do was look up at him dumbly. Their eyes locked momentarily. Finally he spoke. "Coffee?"

His deep, gravely voice, made her heart skip a beat. "Uh...okay."

He led her to the local hangout but neither spoke until they were seated with their cups. "When did you get back?"

"Three weeks ago," she stated looking at her hands clasped around the cup.

"It's hard for me to picture you tending farm animals."

She raised her head and met his gaze head on. "Why is that?" She wasn't sure if he meant it as a challenge or not.

He looked directly into her eyes. "Well, you're a cute, petite woman."

The statement made her heart speed up but she didn't show it. "It's a different world we live in today."

"So I've heard."

"I assure you that I'm fully qualified."

"I have no doubt that you are and I plan to give you a chance to prove it."

"I appreciate your confidence."

He nodded.

She drained her cup and glanced at her watch. "I must be getting back. Thanks for the coffee."

He nodded again.

She had goose bumps as she walked briskly back to the clinic.

Charity attended church regularly with Steve. She had come to the conclusion that she needed to accept Jesus as her Savior but she had a lot of anger in her heart towards her mother and she didn't think that she could forgive her, so she held back. Steve wisely said nothing.

As spring meandered toward summer the weather was glorious. It became apparent to Charity why Montana had been named 'The Big Sky Country'. As she rode through the green pastures towards the mountains the blue sky never seem to end. Charity spent many carefree hours riding Dory. Often she heard the song of a meadowlark or smelled the aroma of pine in the clean fresh air. The cottonwoods, along the river, now stood in full spring dress, their leaves swinging gently in an occasional breeze.

To everyone's surprise Dory allowed Gus to ride her. It happened one morning. He was getting ready to check some of the fences. Gus knocked, then came through the back door into the kitchen.

"What's the matter," Steve asked as he set down his cup of coffee.

"The gator won't start."

"I'll take a look at it."

Charity clipped her cell phone on to her handbag. "Hey why don't you take Dory? I saddled her earlier and was going to take a morning ride but I just got an emergency call and I have to go."

Gus and Steve gazed at her in surprise. "Do ya reckon she'd let me ride er?" Gus asked.

"Yes if you talk softly to her and take charge right away."

"Well I'll give'er a try. Hit'd save time," Gus replied as he went out the door with Steve and Charity behind him.

They observed Gus grab his bag of tools from the gator and walked over to the horse. "Okay girl," he said softly and stroked her neck.

Dory was a little skittish but she allowed him to mount her. She turned and looked at him, then took off like a champion.

"That was nice of you, to lend Gus your horse."

"Well she needs the exercise and I have to go," she stated as she headed back into the house to pick up her bag.

After that, with Charity's blessing, Gus rode Dory often when she wasn't at the ranch. "She's a little wonder, that un. Why I betya she could out run any hoss on this here ranch," Gus told Charity one day.

Charity knew from the start, that Joe didn't approve of lady veterinarians. He would make snide remarks about lady doctors, from time to time, like; "ladies belong in the kitchen." or, "male doctors should wear the pants," then look disapprovingly at her jeans. He also was jealous of any successful person, male or female. His attitude toward the big ranchers was unreasonable. Occasionally he would express his jealousy. They would be tending a downed animal and he would say something like. "Those big ranchers think they own the country."

The first time he made a remark like that, Charity asked him what he meant. "Well I heard that Josh Jordan is going to run for sheriff. It's bad enough that the ranchers own most of the land around here but if Jordan gets to be the sheriff, they'll own the law too." From that time on she ignored his bitter statements. On the other hand, he was good at what he did and saved her both time and sometimes personal injury.

Sporadically Charity would run into Josh. They'd chat on the street, depending on where either of them was heading, at the moment or they'd go for coffee. She could tell that he was attracted to her but he didn't ask her out. She didn't know why.

Her practice was going well. She had a time or two ran into something that stumped her. Each time she called El and he had helped her figure it out.

Chapter 11

Charity was on her way to the clinic, when her cell jingled. "Yes," she said as she drove with her left hand.

"Charity, this is Julie, I have a problem."

"What's up, Julie?"

"My son's babysitter has a bad cold and we both agreed that she shouldn't take care of him, until she's over it. Teddy's other sitter, just had surgery and my folks are out of town, otherwise my mom would take care of him. The only choice I have is to bring him to work with me."

"Well...uh..."

"He's real good, Charity. He's quiet, likes to read and color. He won't be any trouble, I'm sure."

"Okay, Julie."

"Thanks, Charity."

Teddy was a handsome little nine-year-old. His eyes were dark green and sparkled, more so when he laughed or smiled. Bright red hair framed an elfin face, where a perfect bow of a mouth, was symmetrically placed, under a lightly freckled, button nose. His cheeks were plump and rosy. He was well behaved. Whenever Julie was unable to get a setter, with Charity's blessing, Julie would bring him to work with her. He would set behind the counter. Julie had provided him with a TV tray, that he used when he was drawing or coloring. She would store it under her desk, when he wasn't there.

Charity was enthralled by him, from the beginning. But she didn't know how to relate to him. While her teenage girlfriends were babysitting, she had been absorbed in taking care of animals. So not having younger siblings or cousins, while growing up, she had not learned how to interact with young children.

"Miss Wayne, could I visit the animals that you take care of, when the people have to go away?" he asked one day, when Charity had taken a break and was chatting with his mother.

"Now Teddy, don't bug Miss Wayne," Julie told her son, gently.

"He's no bother." Charity smiled down at the boy. "Of course you can Teddy. I have three dogs and a cat back there. Come on, you can see then, now while I'm not busy."

"Oh boy!" he expounded, pushing the tray away and jumping to his feet. "Can I mommy...can I p l e a s e!"

"Well...are you sure, Charity?"

"Of course, I'm sure."

"All right, Teddy, now you be good back there."

"Oh goody!...I'll behave, Mommy," he stated as he followed Charity to where she boarded the animals.

She led him to a room where ten animal cages sat on the floor, each were lined with old newspapers. In the first occupied one, a little black Labrador puppy, not more than nine weeks old, wiggled over to the door of the cage, yipping excitedly and pranced on his hind feet. A card attached to the cage indicated that his name was Benny.

"Oh, he's so cute!" Teddy expounded.

"Yes he is."

"Hi Benny...hi!"

Two other cages were occupied by mature white poodles. One's name was Frankie and the other, Flora. They weren't as exuberant but still acted like they enjoyed having company. They stood on their hind legs, and barked continuously, as they pressed their bodies against the wire doors. The last cage housed a Siamese cat who eyed them cautiously, in a superior manner and remained, independently, in the prone position, at the back of the cage.

Teddy looked at each of the other animals in turn then went back to Benny, who was trying his best, to get someone to let him out to play. "I wish I could play with him, Miss Wayne."

"I know Teddy but I can't let you."

"Why not?"

"If anything happened to you or Benny, my insurance wouldn't cover it."

"I don't understand."

"Well Teddy, I mean that if he should bite you or if he would get hurt in anyway, I could get into trouble for letting, an uninsured person handle one of the animals. Do you understand?"

"Sort of," he stated as they left the room.

A week later, Benny's owner was killed in a car accident. None of the decease's family could or would take Benny or pay the boarding bill. Charity thought about taking him home with her. However the next day, Julie had to bring Teddy to work with her. When Charity got some free time, she spoke to Julie privately.

"Julie may I give Benny to Teddy?"

"Oh...wow! Teddy would be ecstatic!"

"Well?"

"But you could sell him. Isn't he registered?"

"Yes he's got papers. I'm sure the family would get them for me. I would rather give Benny to someone who would love him then sell him to a stranger."

"You know what! Teddy's birthday is next week. Why don't you wait until then?"

"Great idea, we'll have a party!"

That was the beginning of a warm and wonderful boy, dog relationship.

Chapter 12

The Jordans hosted a Forth of July barbecue and invited all their neighbors plus several of the town's people. A local western band entertained on the back porch, off and on throughout the day. A handsome, new American flag waved from a tall pole that stood to the side of the house. Somebody had decorated the back yard with red, white and blue streamers and balloons.

Their father had built the two story county house, twenty years previously. Two bedrooms and a bath occupied the second story. The master bedroom was on the main floor, along with the living room, family and dining room, plus a country kitchen. A small guestroom had also served, as a sewing room for their mother. She had liked bright colors, so the house had been painted gold and sported orange shutters. Orange had been also applied to the trim and the wooden fences.

There were lots of green shrubs in and around the flowerbeds that contained orange and yellow nasturtiums, geraniums and a multicolor of pansies and petunias. A lean-to, next to the stables, functioned as a ranch office. About one hundred horses, had at one time, grazed in the lush pastures but the brothers had let the horse population dwindle, so now there were just three saddle horses. They were strictly cattle ranchers and the quality of their beef, was unsurpassed by anyone.

Josh, Steve, Kerby and Troy Glenn were sitting around a garden table, chatting and drinking lemonade.

"I'm trying to persuade Josh to run for sheriff," Steve informed the others.

"He's got my vote," Kerby stated. He owned the spread to the north of Steve's.

"Mine too," His son Troy, affirmed. "Sheriff Munson is a nice guy but he isn't a good sheriff."

"Well I've been thinking it over." Just then he saw Charity in the crowd. He stood, drink in hand. "Will you gentlemen excuse me, please?"

"Of course," they said in unison.

Josh worked his way through the crowd, greeting people as he went. Finally, he caught up with Charity. She was talking to Stella, Kerby's wife. Both women turned and greeted him.

"It was nice of you to do all this," Stella stated, indicating she meant the party, gesturing with her hand.

"Thank you. Please enjoy yourself. The food should be ready soon." The delicious aroma of cooking meat, blended with spices and sauces, hung in the air.

Stella excused herself and headed toward a tub of cold beverages.

"How's your practice?"

"Good. Doc Ross has been kind enough to cover the clinic for me from time to time and Joe and Julie know their jobs. I was lucky to move into an established practice."

"Yes you were."

She changed the subject "Are you going to take the challenge?"

"What do you mean?" Her soft brown eyes made him feel weak in the knees. It was unsettling.

"Are you going to run for sheriff?"

"Maybe." He had to look away, so he wouldn't betray his emotions.

"So why are you hesitating?"

"Might make enemies."

"I see what you mean."

The band was playing The Yellow Rose of Texas. Some guy was singing, they both heard the refrain, "but the yellow rose of Texas is the only gal for me."

"Personally I think Montana gals, are just as good." He looked back at her with new resolve. Their eyes were locked.

"Why is that?"

"They're hardy. This is a rough country."

"Some gals are tougher then you think."

He sensed that there was a message in there somewhere. He continued to hold her gaze and took awhile to answer. "I hope so."

There were a great variety of foods that included barbecued beef, pork and chicken, cole slaw, baked beans, potato salad, corn on the cob and biscuits. Apple and cherry pies didn't have to wait long for the ice cream freezers, to finish their toppings. Besides lemonade, there was an assortment of sodas, plus coffee and tea. Later after everyone else was eating the main course, Cal found Josh tending one of the ice cream freezers. "Aren't you going to have something to eat?"

Josh smiled over at his younger brother. "Yup soon."

"Hey, I've already stuffed myself. I can take over if you like."

"You always were a fast eater."

He grinned. "Yaw and you're a slow mover."

Josh considered his response. He sensed where Cal was going with their conversation. "So?"

"I'm not blind. I see you making calf eyes at Charity."

Josh's smile faded. "I didn't know it showed."

"Most people probably wouldn't notice but I've lived with you all my life. I know you fairly well."

"Uh... she's quite a gal."

"Then way don't you ask her out?"

He hesitated. "I've wanted too but she might not like it here and move back to San Diego."

"You mean, like her mother did?"

"Yup."

"I understand."

"I haven't given up. I'll see how she withstands this coming winter."

"That sounds like a good plan but what if someone else snatches her up, while you're trying to make up your mind."

Josh thought for a moment before answering. Then he looked Cal squarely in the eyes. "Then it wasn't meant to be."

Troy found Clover and sat down next to her. They indulged in small talk for awhile. "Would you have dinner with me sometime." he asked, at last.

He had taken her by surprise. "Uh...I...don't know... Actually I couldn't."

He looked away.

"I'm sorry," she said kindly.

Presently he raised his head and gazed directly into her eyes. "I've got something to say to you," he stated, with new boldness.

"What's that, Troy?"

"I've been stuck on you since we were kids."

She was speechless.

"I figured that I might as well tell you and if you change your mind about that date, you just let me know."

"I will Troy."

When the sun went down Josh and Cal presented a fireworks display. Some were just splashes of brilliant colors, while others were patriotic. There were eagles, American flags, and the statue of liberty.

Chapter 13

Dust kicked up beneath Dory's hooves as she trotted. The earth was thirsty and the pasture grass needed water. Even the needles on the hardy Juniper bushes were brittle. July's rainfall had dropped fifty percent below normal and in the hot August days it was nonexistent. Ranchers and farmers alike worried about not having enough hay for their stock during the long winter.

Vegetables were dying in the fields. The fruit yield was poor and what was produced was dry and tasteless.

Charity reined Dory to a stop and stroked her neck as she surveyed the expanse. "It looks bad, girl." Dory turned her head and looked at Charity then faced forward and nodded her head up and down like she understood. Charity smiled sadly. "Sometimes I think you do know what I'm saying."

"Let's go girl," she said finally urging her toward the river. They had gone that way many times, so she gave Dory her head. Each time she checked the river, it was lower.

The wind was in her face. Then in the distance she saw a man standing by a horse and as he turned his head, the sun picked up a shiny object on his hatband, causing her to squint. "Whoa girl," she said, stopping her again. As she watched, he crouched down on the ground. The next thing she saw brought terror to her heart. Flames began to shoot up, as the man jumped on his horse and rode off. "Oh my God!" She pulled her cell phone off of her belt and called Steve's cell but he didn't answer.

"Oh no!" Panic stricken she punched in the house phone number. It ran four times before Clover answered it.

"Hello."

"Clover the range is on fire! Do you know what to do?" Charity's heart was pounding rapidly.

"Yes! Where?"

"Just west of the river. The wind is blowing from the west. The fire is moving fast!"

"Okay, I'll get right on it!"

"Good, I'll stay here as long as I can. If anyone wants to call me about it they can."

"Right." Clover ended the call.

Within minutes Steve had sent some ranch hands to the fire cache, while he and others were on their way with shovels.

It seemed like an eternity had passed, when her cell buzzed. "Hello."

"Charity, this is your dad."

"Oh Dad, where are you?"

"We're only a few miles away."

"I can hear the rumble of the trucks... Oh Dad, please hurry. I'm terrified!"

"We're coming as fast as we can."

"I know you are but I feel so alone!"

"Just hold on, girl."

Numerous jackrabbits, of different sizes, came into view, frantically running for their lives. Then prairie dogs, families of foxes and a mule deer doe jumped up from her hiding place, followed by her yearling and dashed toward Charity, away from the flames.

Charity glanced from time to time in the direction

of the house and finally she could see a cloud of dust moving toward her. She felt some relief but she knew that they had a tough job ahead of them. At last she could see Steve's gator in the lead. From out a dust cloud, five trucks appeared. Several ranch hands were in the back of each truck including Billy and Gus. Two more gators and the jeep were behind the trucks. Each man had a handkerchief tied around his neck, covering his nose and mouth. The water tanker was in the rear. The wild animals met them and separated making a path for the coming vehicles.

Soon some of the men began to dig a trench with their pulaskis, while others threw shovels full of dirt on the flames, to smother them. The tanker was situated and the water hose begin to attack the blaze. Then Charity could hear a helicopter but the smoke was too thick for her to spot it until it was just above the fire. The huge scoop hanging from the bottom of the chopper dumped water, from the river, onto the flames. The smoke billowed high in the sky, as the flames seem to disappear, only to rise again.

At first it looked like the fire was winning. The men were working feverishly. Charity's heart continued to pound. She thought about praying but she didn't think she was in good enough standing with God, so at first she sat like a stone and just watched. The crew had managed to stomp out the flames to the north and south but the fire was lapping up everything in its path as it dashed east.

Her heart pounded faster when some of the flames leaped over the trench. "Oh dear God! Please hear my prayer! I'm sorry that I've put you off. Please forgive me! And stop the fire!" The men worked franticly to halt the runaway flames, with the shovels and water from the tanker. At last the fire was contained on the east side of the trench. "Oh thank you God!" she sobbed.

Sometime later Kerby and Troy Glenn arrived, with most of their hands, as did Josh and cal. They relieved the men who had been dumping dirt on the flames, as several were coughing from the smoke and needed to breathe in some fresh air. From the time that Charity spotted the fire, Dory got more and more skittish. She kept turning to look at Charity, as if to say; "let's get out of here." Charity however was able to control her. Each time Dory would look at her, Charity would say something like. "Its okay girl," and pat her on the neck.

Within a half-hour after the other ranches had arrived, a miracle took place. The fire was out! Simultaneously a cheer went up from the men! At Charity's urging Dory galloped toward them. She reined Dory in, leaped to the ground, when she saw Steve and rushed into his arms. "Oh Dad, I was so scared!" She said breathlessly.

"Me too, daughter, me too!"

She looked up at him then glanced around. "Did anyone get hurt?"

"No thank God. Did you recognize the rat who started this?"

"No. He was too far away. He was nothing but a black form against the trees."

"What did his horse look like?"

"It was dark, maybe brown."

"Did you see which way he went?"

"He rode east and disappeared into the trees."

"I'm so glad that you saw him. That fire could have wiped me out, if it would have spread. It could have burned down the buildings, including the house and possibly taken some of our lives, as well as the animals."

Charity shivered. "I know Dad. Who ever started that fire is a contemptible person. He has no regard for human life. He wants this ranch and it looks like, he'll stop at nothing to get it."

"I suppose I should report this to the sheriff but I don't have much confidence in him."

Most of the men had dropped to the ground, some sitting down, others lying on their backs. Two or three were smoking cigarettes. Still others were wiping sweat, dirt and soot off their faces and necks with their handkerchiefs.

Sometime later two trucks were parked, one in front of the other, on a lonely stretch of country road. A man got out of the truck, in the back and climbed into the passenger side, of the other one. "Howdy," he said after he closed the door.

"Don't howdy me!"

"What's the matter?"

"You know very well, what the matter is."

He sighed. "I know, I know, Charity saw me."

"Setting that fire was stupid."

"Hey, if she hadn't seen me, you'd be close to having Steve's ranch, by now."

He shook his head in disgust. "Or I could have been wiped out."

"What do you mean?"

"If the wind had shifted, I would have lost everything."

"They said on the weather forecast that the wind was going to be blowing from the west all day."

"Hello! How many times have they been wrong? Huh!"

"Well they weren't," he mumbled.

He turned and glared at his companion. "I'm only going to tell you this once, so listen up. From now on, I decide what you are to do and when. Do you understand?"

"Yaw," he answered, under his breath.

"What did you say?" He demanded.

He turned and glared back. "I said yes."

"Good so long as we understand each other. We are going to have to wait for a while until things cool off. When the time is right I'll let you know. And another thing, if you have to get in touch with me call my cell phone, from a pay phone, let it ring twice, then hang up. I'll meet you here at the usual time"

"Why?"

"Because, if you call my cell, from your phone and later if the law should check my phone, they might wonder what you and I have in common."

"I don't get it."

He sighed and rolled his eyes up. "Look, we aren't exactly in the same social set."

A week later the heavens opened up and the earth was blessed with three inches of rain in forty-eight hours. The ranchers now had another worry on their hands, as the rain continued to fall. If the deluge persisted, the rivers would overflow their banks and instead of fires, they would have to deal with a flood. All the landowners started to prepare for the possible disaster. Fatalists hoped that Mother Nature would slacken her fury, while people of faith turned to God. As the thunder cracked and lightening streaked across the sky, Steve and Charity drove to church. "You must be troubled about the possibility of flooding," Charity shouted over the din.

"Of course, if the heavy rainfall persists, it may well cause as much damage as a fire. Homes, farmland, stock and people might be washed away; years of hard work and dreams gone."

"Oh Dad what will you do!"

"Be prepared and then leave it up to God."

"But Dad, if you prayed and asked God for help; why would you need be prepared? Isn't that lack of faith?"

After he pulled into the church parking lot and stopped the engine he turned to her. "Have you heard the story of Noah and the Ark?"

"Yes."

"What did God tell Noah to do?"

She smiled. "To build the ark and be prepared."

"Enough said," he stated, ending the conversation and climbing out of the truck.

Three days later the rain stopped as suddenly as it had started. It had caused little damage. When the sun came out the ground flourished. It was apparent that most of the crops would produce a fairly good yield. The populace was overjoyed. The fatalists applauded Mother Nature while others gave God the glory.

Chapter 14

It was a magnificent late August day. The giant orb of a sun, hung in the bluest of skies, directly overhead, in all its glory. A few white, fleecy clouds drifted through the firmament. Only a gentle breeze stirred the pine and maple trees. Rainbows of color extended throughout the flowerbeds, where numerous shades of irises, begonias, petunias and roses, shared the soil with orange moss roses, baby breath and white alyssum. The bouquet as Charity passed by was breathtaking. Only when she neared the grills, laden with plump, juicy hotdogs, was the aroma of the meat able to compete with the flowers. Amazingly they blended well. *Probably because I'm famished.*

"Would you like one?" A stocky, pleasant looking man asked her.

"Yes please." Her mouth watered as she watched him pick up an evenly browned, succulent, frankfurter and place it into a toasted bun. An adjoining table provided condiments and she spread an ample amount of mustard on the meat. It was as delicious as it smelled.

She munched on it, as she moved toward a small platform, across the park, on which Cal and Josh were sitting, behind a card table. Both wore western cut clothes, as did most of the Montana ranchers. Josh had on a black cotton shirt, that she noticed later, made his eyes even darker. Cal had chosen a blue, one that had black cowboy hats embroidered on it. In back of them, the same band that had entertained at their Fourth of July party was alternating between patriot and country renditions.

A banner with Joss Jordan for Sheriff, printed on it, hung across the top of a small cabana, which shaded the platform. A crowd was gathering on the plush green lawn. Cal was the first to see her and he waved, then Josh spotted her, stepped down and meandered toward her. Her heart flipped over! At that moment she knew and the knowledge unnerved her. She was unable to finish her meal. He smiled as he drew near. *Okay so I love him!...I can do this. I can stay calm.*

He took her hand. "You came. Does that mean I get your vote?"

Her heart beat faster. It took all of her strength to keep from stuttering. "I'll let you know, after I hear what you have to say." She forced a confident smile.

He was taken aback. He paused and chuckled "Fair enough...You're direct, I like that."

At that moment Cal was by his side. He smiled at Charity then turned to Josh. "Sorry to break this up but I think we should start."

Josh looked around at the throng of people. "Yup." He glanced back at her. " I'll see you later," he said as he squeezed her hand. Both men made their way back to the platform.

Charity started to tremble. *It's a good thing that he left me when he did. I might have said something stupid.* She had never been in love before and it was the first situation, since she was a teen, that she didn't know how handle. It was also the first time that she wished that she and Clover were close so she could confide in her. *I need a woman's point of view.* In the past she had been able to talk most anything over with her mother but now...

A couple of teenage boys were passing out fliers to the crowd. One of the boys handed her one.

Cal stood up holding a wireless microphone. The band stopped playing and he began to speak. "Ladies and gentlemen, as most of you know, my name is Cal Jordan. I grew up in this community. But I'm not here to talk about myself. I am here to ask you to vote for a fine man, a man I have known all my life, my brother Josh." Someone in the crowd whistled, some clapped. "As you might have guessed, I'm prejudiced so I have asked our good friend and neighbor, Steve Wayne to tell you all what an outstanding guy my brother is and why he would make a great sheriff." Three more persons whistled and the applause grew louder.

Steve stepped up on the platform and took the microphone from Cal. The people roared and clapped for some time but at last they grew quiet. Charity swelled with pride to find out how much her dad was thought of, by his neighbors.

Steve cleared his throat. "I didn't realize that I was that well known." There was another brief applause. "But like Cal, I'm not here to talk about myself. So I'll get right to the point. I think most of you aren't happy with the present official." Someone yelled "NO!" A few booed. Steve continued. "Oh he's a good man but he's not strong enough. Now Josh Jordan is not only a tough sort of guy, he's smart. He has a college degree in animal husbandry from the university but what most of you don't know is, that he minored in law-enforcement. He also maintained an 'A' average, all the way through. Josh is honest and fair-minded. If he were the sheriff he wouldn't decide on anything until he had all the facts. Those are some of the reasons that I have encouraged him to run for the office. I'm asking you to get better acquainted with Josh and then vote for him in November. Now let me introduce my friend and neighbor and next sheriff, Joshua Jordan." As Josh took the microphone the crowd started to clap, and whistle, again. He smiled and waved until they were silent.

"My friends tell me, that I'm a man of few words. So...to prove them right, all I have to say is, that I would appreciate your vote this November and if I am elected I promise to do the best job that I can. Thanks folks." The people cheered and applauded for some time. Josh handed the microphone back to Cal and when it was quiet again he spoke. "Folks, here on the table are some fliers," he held one up, "that explain more in detail, what Josh stands for and some of the things that he would do, if elected. If you haven't gotten one yet, please feel free to help yourself and do take advantage of the hotdogs provided by Juicy Franks. Also there are tubs of cold drinks out there, so don't go away hungry or thirsty."

Charity found a trash can and disposed of the half-eaten hot dog. Near by she spied a tub of sodas and selected a seven-up.

Chapter 15

"Charity, you're not yourself tonight. Is something wrong?" Steve asked when they were finishing up with their dinner.

She sighed. "Yes, I got a call from Mom today."

"Was it bad news?"

"No...uh."

"Then what?"

"She wants to come and visit me."

Clover looked up from her dinner plate. They were all silent for a moment.

"Is that a problem?" Steve asked.

"Well, she'll stay at a motel, of course but..."

"Why does she have to stay in town? She'd be welcome here."

"But...wouldn't that be awkward?"

"Maybe, a little but we're all adults. When is she coming?"

"Not until after the fair."

"Good. We're all going to be pretty busy during that time."

Charity had never been to a fair and rodeo. She could feel the excitement as she walked beside Steve. Clover had gone off with friends, to watch the horse races. A western band could be heard in the background. They passed by where some men were frying hamburgers, as several people waited in line. Her mouth watered as they neared a concession that was selling elephant ears, as fast as they could make them. *I'll get one later.*

"Where are we going first?" She asked, looking

over the program of events.

"I wanted to see how my Hereford steer, Ditto fared in the competition. They should be through judging by now."

She followed him into a shed where different types of bovine were stalled. She wrinkled her nose at the odor of manure, mingled with hay. Steve grinned widely when they found Ditto, as there was a blue ribbon taped to his stall. She hugged Steve then he turned back and rubbed Ditto's head. "I knew you were a winner, boy."

"Well, what do we do next, Dad?"

"Lets find out how Clover's huckleberry jam placed, then we'll check the program together so you can pick out what interests you."

"Okay."

As they walked down the fairway they met Joe. He was eating a hotdog.

Steve reached out and shook Joe's hand. "Glad to see you."

She could see Joe bristle. However he returned the handshake. "I...I have to go. I'll see you at work, Charity."

"Sure Joe." They watched him walk away.

"I wonder what he's so prickly about," Steve commented later.

"I didn't know if you realized it or not but he's jealous of any successful person, especially the big ranchers around here."

Steve shrugged his shoulders and said nothing.

Unfortunately Clover's jam came in third. There were many entries. Several had blue ribbons attached to them. *My sister dear, is going to be harder than ever to live with, for awhile.*

Charity chose the art and clothing pavilion and she then followed Steve through the horse stalls. They enjoyed a western band as they rested on some bleachers.

After they each had a juicy hamburger, they split an elephant ear.

Later when they entered the rodeo grandstand, she spied, Josh, some distance away, with a tall, willowy blond. Her heart sank. She chided herself but she couldn't help how she felt. What had started out to be a memorable day, had now turned to ashes. *Well Charity, you assumed that he felt the same way you did, but now you know that he doesn't.* For the rest of the day, her mind was in a fog. She sat nimbly through the roping, bronco and bull riding contests. Later she couldn't recall any of it.

Chapter 16

Jean felt a little apprehensive as she deplaned and walked down the concourse. She didn't know how Charity would receive her. Ever since the day that she had told Charity the truth about her dad, she had been depressed. Jean was afraid that she had lost her daughter forever. She had to admit that the last few times that they had talked on the phone, Charity seemed a bit warmer. Also Charity sounded like she was glad that her mother was coming to visit.

Sooner or later I'm going to have to face Steve. Her apprehension grew at the thought of it.

The waiting crowd was small and she spied Charity right away. When they faced each other she momentarily hesitated then she hugged her. To her relief and joy Charity hugged her back. "It's good to see you, dear," Jean stated.

Charity wasn't ready for any endearing words, so she just smiled and changed the subject. "Did you have a good flight?"

Jean felt that the hug they had shared was positive progress. "It was delightful. I sat next to a lady who was in her eighties and we had a lovely visit. She has been a Montana ranch wife for over sixty years. She was visiting her granddaughter in San Diego and is now on her way back home to her ranch near Glendive."

"I'm glad that you found someone to talk to, Mom. It helps to pass the time on a long flight," she stated as they neared the luggage carousel.

"I didn't make reservations for you at a motel like you ask me to because there are plenty of vacancies now that the fair is over. Besides Dad said that you could stay at the ranch," she stated as she put Jean's luggage in the back of the truck.

"What! You're not serious?"

"Yes, we are all adults, to quote him;" she quipped as she backed out of the parking lot.

"I don't know Charity. It's going to be tough enough when I do see him...but to stay at the ranch...I'm not sure I can do that," she said after a long pause.

"Why don't you give it a try? You can always move to a motel if it proves to be uncomfortable."

"I don't want to cause extra work for anyone."

"Don't worry about that. Dad has a lady who comes in five days a week to clean and do the laundry."

"Well..."

"I told you about Clover. She does the cooking most of the time."

"I wonder how she'll react to me."

"It's hard to say. It depends on whether she thinks that you're a threat to her security or not."

Jean looked around as Charity drove. "There have been a lot of changes since I was here."

"Well it's been over twenty years, Mom."

"I know. I haven't seen a landmark yet that I recognize."

"You probably would if you were in the old section of town. Maybe I can drive you down there before you go back."

"That would be nice."

"I'll show you my clinic tomorrow if you like."

"Sure."

"You can go in with me in the morning." They were out in the country by now.

"Okay."

They approached a produce stand by the side of the road. Jean read out loud, "Fresh corn, tomatoes, spaghetti squash, potatoes and pumpkins. Looks like the drought didn't hurt the crops."

"It would have done a lot of damage if it hadn't rained."

"Wow!" Jean exclaimed when they turned down the lane to the house.

"What's the matter?"

"This is all different. The place that I remember was an old farmhouse."

"Yes, Dad said that he had the new house built ten years ago."

"I'm nervous, Charity. I don't know if I can do this," Jean stated, before they reached the house.

"Mom, Dad's busy overseeing. They're harvesting the oats. There have been some problems. The combine broke down. It took a day for Dad to get parts and get it working again. Then the man who was running it ended up in the hospital with acute appendicitis. One of the other hands is operating it now. So Dad's been working fourteen hours a day. You can easily avoid him."

Jean sighed. "Nothing's changed." However relief came over her.

"Usually it's different now, according to Dad."

"Like what?"

"Well since he built up the ranch he has more time, as he has a foreman, Billy who has taken over a lot of Dad's duties and he has good ranch hands.

However he did say that during harvest time he is the busiest. But they should be done with the oats soon."

"Like when?"

"In about three more days, by then maybe you'll be more relaxed about seeing him."

"I doubt it."

Charity parked the truck. "Come on, I'll take you to meet Clover. She's probably in the kitchen. I'll come back for your luggage."

"Okay," Jean said as she climbed out of the truck.

Three days later it happened. Clover was in the habit of leaving coffee in an insulated carafe in the kitchen for anyone in the house. It would stay hot for a long time and not turn bitter. It was mid-morning. Charity had gone to the clinic and Clover was out riding Ginger. Jean poured herself a mug of coffee and was on her way back to the dining room. After bending over expense accounts for two hours, Steve was ready for a break, so at the moment Jean started through the swinging door, Steve was coming from the other way and he ran into her and spilled her coffee.

"Oh!" she screeched. Luckily neither one got burned.

"Jean! I'm sorry!"

They looked intently at each other in silence. The coffee was forgotten. It was like the pages of time had rolled backward. She was lost in his deep blue eyes. Her heart was pounding. No other man had ever made such an impact on her...ever.

At last she found her voice. "Uh...I'll clean this up." She looked down at the floor.

"No...let me."

"Don't be silly."

"I ran into you. I should do it."

"Okay." She inhaled deeply and let it out, as she backed into the kitchen.

Steve took some paper towels and wiped up the spill while Jean poured him a mug of coffee adding a lump of sugar and refilling her mug. Then they both sat down at the kitchen table. "I'm surprised that you remember how I like my coffee," he stated after he took a sip.

She didn't know how to respond. She stared into her mug. *Well what do I say that I remember a lot of things about you...and that I almost came crawling back, more than once?*

He cleared is throat. "Uh...how was your trip?"

Well at least you were able to say something, how ever trite. "It was okay." *And I didn't do any better.* She forced herself to meet his gaze.

"Are you still in real estate?"

"Yes."

At that moment Clover came through the back door. Jean relaxed a little. Steve and Clover started talking about the horses. Jean finished her coffee and excused herself.

One evening Jean and Gus had a long visit. He was the only ranch hand that had been in Steve's employ when she and Steve were married. She liked his crusty ways.

By the time Jean left, she and Steve were more comfortable with each other.

Chapter 17

Steve stared out the window, unable to concentrate. She had been gone for over a month. The last time she left, some twenty years earlier, she had taken most of his heart with her. His faith in God and afterward his Sweet Flower's gentle ways had saved him. His love for her had been an easy, serene love. But what he had felt for Jean had been fierce and overpowering. Much to his surprise it had returned with as much force as it had originally. *I'm a fool.* He chided himself. He shook his head. *I have to get her out of my mind.* He left his office, took a soda out of the refrigerator and sat down at the kitchen table. He had been stunned by her youthfulness. She hadn't changed much. She was still slim. Her dark brown hair probably had help staying that way. But those warm brown eyes still moved him. He tried to think of something else but it was no use. *She's not going to come back here. If she couldn't stand Montana back then, she's not going to like it any better now. Besides we're different people now...twenty some years different.* He finished his soda, abandoned the office work and saddled Midnight. He headed him west toward the river. Orange, yellow and gold met his eyes. Soon kids would be trick or treating.

He startled a bevy of bob white quail and watched them scurry out of Midnight's way. Before he got to the river he reined his horse to a stop. In a moment of weakness, he had gotten Jean's phone number off of Charity's cell and programmed it into his phone. When her name came up he didn't give

99

himself a moment to think about it. He pressed the call button down. Steve was halfway relieved when he got her voice-mail. He didn't leave a message. *You idiot, what would you say to her anyway? Come back and be my wife again?* He knew he ought to talk it over with Evan but he wasn't ready to, not yet. *What if she came back and then left again? You'd be done for, you poor slob. At least now you have your sanity.*

Steve tried to get absorbed in the beauty of the day as he rode along. Soon he was at the river. He dismounted and sat down on a log. The rushing water had a soothing effect on him. A few of the trees were already barren. He silently watched, as autumn toned leaves, continued to fall, some to the ground; others were picked up by a breath of wind and carried away while a number of them dropped into the river and floated to another destination.

When the cattle had been driven down from the northern slopes, a buyer arrived and purchased calves that had been born the previous year. Some weighed in at six hundred pounds. After the transaction was complete a company with trucks came and hauled them to feed lots, where they waited to be transported to their journey's end.

Halloween came and went. Eight days later Josh won the election by a land-slide.

Winter came in harshly. Steve didn't have much time to think about Jean. By Thanksgiving, the thermometer had dropped to thirty degrees below zero. He knew it would test Charity's endurance. Steve didn't want her to fail. He prayed that she would want to stay. *Please God, if I can't have Jean, let me keep Charity.*

Icicles hung from the buildings and the trees. Intricate patterns of frost decorated the windows. Fluffy white snow covered the ground. More fell each day, keeping the snowplows and sand trucks busy. The thermometer registered forty below when the Christmas holidays arrived. Steve's days were long and hard. He was sure that he had made the right decision about Jean.

One of Steve's two year old bulls, he named Basil, gave every indication that he was going to be an outstanding stud. It wasn't long before Steve was using him to service some of his cows. Then he decided to use him strictly for artificial insemination, which proved to be profitable and more than offset his losses due to the black cohosh.

Chapter 18

It was a cold winter day. Charity was glad that it was Sunday afternoon and she was enjoying the warmth of the fireplace as she curled up with a good book that she had wanted to read. She hadn't finished the first chapter when her cell buzzed. *Shoot! I hope it's not an emergency.* Unfortunately some lady was in hysterics about her poodle that had been hit by a car. She hurried to put on her winter coat and boots. About then Clover walked into the room.

"Are you going out?"

"Yes, I should be back in time for supper," she stated as she went out the door.

When Charity drove into the clinic parking lot, a tearful lady stepped out of a car holding the injured animal. Charity was momentarily taken aback as she was the same willowy blond that Charity had seen with Josh at the rodeo.

Inside she had her place the dog on the examining table.

Charity informed her, after she had thoroughly examined the dog and taken x-rays, that she didn't think her pet had any internal injuries but that her right front leg was fractured.

"Oh no, my poor baby!"

"It's a simple fracture. It should heal just fine. However I'll have to put her leg in a walking cast...Miss...?"

"Hannah...Hannah Storm. Her name is Baby... You're Charity. Josh Jordan has told me a lot about you."

Charity's heart missed a beat. "Uh...that's nice."

Charity went to work and with sedation for Baby and Hannah's help, Baby did okay. "I'm going to give her a shot of antibiotic so she won't get an infection," she explained to Hannah, as she drew up a syringe of yellow liquid.

"She's going to be a little groggy for awhile." She handed Hannah a small bottle. "These are some pain pills. Give her one twice a day, one in the morning and one at night in some food until they are gone. Call me if you have any problems."

Hannah picked Baby up. "Josh was right. You are a good doctor." Her soft violet eyes were now dry. "Thank you, so much."

"You're welcome, Hannah," Charity said, as she headed towards her truck.

Why did she turn out to be so nice? I was all set to hate her.

Charity and Josh still met for coffee. Sometimes he would come by the clinic. They had built-up a camaraderie. As the families were friendly, they frequently ate meals together. She worked at keeping her feelings in check, so by the time she met Hannah she had developed the skill.

Her hours were not her own. She got called night and day. 'So and so' had a downed cow or a prize mare was having a difficult delivery or a stud bull had tangled with barbwire. By January she had figured out why her mother had not been able to cope on a Montana ranch, especially a struggling ranch, twenty years previously. But Charity was made of stronger stuff. She wasn't about to give up. The majority of the time she loved the cold, crisp air, the white carpet of fresh snow, the crystal icicles and the artistry of Jack Frost. But the first time her hands and feet were numb from the extreme cold and later when they stung as they thawed out a little doubt crept into her mind. However Charity learned to dress like she was going to the North Pole. And to live with her truck heater that didn't get warm, when it was more than thirty-five below zero; during short trips and most of her trips were short.

Jean called her at least once a week. She felt warmer towards her mother but she hadn't forgiven her.

Steve and Kerby Glenn had been casual friends for years. Sporadically the two families dined together.

Steve started dating a widow that he met at church. She and her sons had a farm up towards Kings Hill Pass. Charity didn't like her and she couldn't understand why. Barbara, the widow was a nice lady. Charity thought that Clover was jealous but it was hard to tell as Clover could hide her feelings, when she wanted to.

January and February drug on. Finally with the arrival of March there was a break in the weather. To Charity's delight she heard a robin then she saw him perched on the corral fence. The snow had started to melt and it was much like the year before when she had first come to Montana.

She and Josh continued to run into one another from time to time. He never mentioned Hannah and Charity thought that it would be remiss if she did. They often dined together either at Josh and Cal's or at the Wayne ranch. Sometimes they would all go out to eat. Charity thought it was strange that Hannah was never present during those occasions.

One day Josh stopped by the clinic as she was closing up. They chatted as the meandered over to the coffee shop. Later there was silence while they both sipped their coffee. Then he surprised her. "I have tickets to the rancher's banquet Friday night. Want to go?"

Her heart leaped. "But...but..."

"But what?"

"What about Hannah?"

He stared at her nonplus. "Oh I get it," he said at last. "You think Hannah's my girlfriend."

"Isn't she?"

He smiled sadly. "Hannah's my cousin. Her husband Cliff died of cancer last August. We had her come and stay with us for as long as she needed to. I think it did her good to get away from everything that reminded her of him for awhile. She stayed with us until the holidays and then she decided to go back home. His family lives there."

Relief washed over her. She felt giddy. "Where is that?"

"Great Falls."

She finished her coffee and waited for him to ask her again but much to her chagrin he didn't. At last she spoke up. "What time, Friday?"

"Six o'clock," he answered with a grin.

Joe had continued to make disparaging remarks about anyone that he thought was successful, particularly the big ranchers. However after Charity had taken over the clinic for about eight months, she sensed that she had gained his respect. Joe had watched her steadfast determination, as they both trudged through that first winter. The snide remarks toward her stopped.

Chapter 19

Steve had watched his elder daughter closely and with each passing winter month he had been more pleased. He had planned to change his will but had waited to see if she would be able to deal with Montana winters, if not, he would have the will state that the ranch would be sold and the money divided between both the girls. Steve was happy it would stay in the family. He knew that Charity and Clover didn't get along but he prayed that in time that would change.

In late March, Steve called both girls into his office. "This must be serious, Dad," Clover stated.

"I wanted you to know that I've changed my will."

Clover sat straight up and stared at her father.

"Relax Clover. I've left the ranch to both of you."

Instantly Clover got control of her emotions. From then on she remained stoic.

"When the time comes, I think Clover can run the ranch, with Billy's help. Besides Charity, you have your practice.

Charity glanced at Clover. "I haven't any problem with that. I don't know the first thing about running a ranch."

From that day forward Clover barely acknowledged Charity's presence.

Steve always kept about five hundred dollars in a drawer in his desk, replacing it as he needed. The habit had started soon after he had built the new house. If he wanted quick cash it was there. Even after he obtained a debit card he had continued the practice. One day, when he was getting ready to go to town, he opened the drawer to get out a fifty dollar bill. The money was gone. He gaped in disbelief at the empty drawer. *Maybe I stuck it in a different drawer by mistake.* But after a thorough search of his desk he knew that someone had taken it. *But who, not Charity, Clover or Molly. No one else has been in this office, lately.* He was stumped. When he went to the store, he used his debit card.

He always took his watch off at night and placed it on the night stand by his bed. Not until he took his morning shower and dressed would he put it back on his wrist. Three days after his money was missing, his watch wasn't where he had left it the night before. *What the...! Maybe I put it someplace else. I've been distracted lately.* But after he had thoroughly searched the bedroom, he knew that somebody had taken it. *But who? Molly's been with me for years and the girls wouldn't take it, so who...? This is bizarre. Whoever did it had to have picked it up either in the night or while I was in the shower....I guess someone could have come in the house during the night. We better start locking the doors... However I'm not going to say anything about the watch for awhile...*

That day Steve bought a new watch. And had four of the front and back door keys made, so he would have one extra and gave one of each to Charity, Clover and Molly and instructed then to keep the doors locked from then on.

A week later when he sat down at his desk he realized that what was happening, had to be an inside job, because a picture of Sweet Flower on her favorite pinto Patches was gone. The empty frame gaped back at him from where it had sat for fifteen years. He jumped to his feet and started around the room, examining all the pictures one by one, on the bookcase and the walls. Every picture of Sweet Flower was gone, removed from their frames. Even the photos that they had taken together were gone.

He was extremely troubled. Steve dropped into his chair and lowered his head into his hands. For a long time he stayed in that position, not wanting to deal with the problem, he just wanted it to go away.

A knock at his office door jarred him out of his oblivion. "Yes."

"Mister Steve...uh...," Molly stated after she opened the door.

"What is it Molly. You look like you've seen a ghost."

"I think you had better come with me...I can't tell you...uh..."

He sighed. "Okay." Steve followed her up the stairs and into Charity's room.

"Mister Steve...I almost didn't show you this but..." She was wringing her hands.

"What...Molly?" he asked glancing around the room.

"Come over here, Mister Steve," she said walking over to the chest of drawers. She pulled the top drawer open. There lying on some underwear was Steve's watch, Sweet Flower's pictures and several bills.

Steve was thunderstruck.

"I was putting her laundry away when I spied the corner of a picture sticking out from under a garment. When I pulled the picture out I felt something hard so I started searching through her things and uncovered your watch, the rest of the pictures and the money. "Mister Steve, I'm sorry," she said, wringing her hands again.

"It's all right, Molly. You did the right thing," he said at last.

Tears filled her eyes. She looked down at the floor.

"Please don't tell anyone about this. Do you understand? Molly."

She sniffled and raised her head. "Yes, Mister Steve. I won't tell a soul."

When Charity came home from the clinic, Steve met her at the door.

"What's the matter, Dad? You look menacing."

"Come with me," he commanded.

"Sure Dad. This must be serious."

Wordlessly he led her to her room and showed her the drawer. At the same time Clover came down the hall and stood in the doorway.

It was Charity's turn to be thunderstruck.

"What have you got to say about this Charity?" he asked harshly.

"I...I...don't know what to say....I."

"What does this mean?" he asked between his teeth. "That you're jealous of a dead woman?"

She turned and met his gaze. "Dad I didn't do this."

He shook his head. "Charity, the evidence speaks for itself."

Tears pooled her eyes. "Dad, I didn't take your money, your watch or the pictures. I swear."

"So who did?"

At that time Charity saw Clover, still standing in the doorway. "I have a pretty good idea who did."

Steve looked at Clover then back at Charity. "Are you implying that Clover did?"

"Yes, she has tried to get rid of me every since I came here."

Steve was quiet for a moment, then he turned on Charity. "Young lady, it's bad enough that you did this but to try and blame Clover for it makes it even worse!"

Charity flashed Clover an intense glare. "Well it looks like you won, Clover." She then pulled her suitcase off of the closet shelf and stated grabbing things at random and cramming then into the bag.

Without another word, Steve turned and marched down the stairs and into his office, slamming the door behind him.

Chapter 20

Yes! I got rid of that 'witch of a white eyes'!
Clover literally danced down the stairs and into the
kitchen. *Dad will probably change his will back to
the way it was now.* She hummed a tune while she
fixed supper.

She wasn't prepared for what the future had in
store. That evening Steve didn't come out of his
office until long after she had gone to bed. She had
opened his door and told him that supper was ready.
He had raised his head up from off of his arms
which were resting on his desk, just long enough to
tell her that he wasn't hungry. She was a little
stunned at first but after she thought about it she
came to the conclusion that his reaction had been
normal and that his despair would pass in a few
days. How wrong she was. Two weeks went by.
Steve had gone into a deep depression. He never
smiled and rarely spoke. Clover was forced to take
over some of the overseeing chores. That was the
only good thing about the situation. In the future she
might need the experience.

Gus quit talking to her. In fact he even quit
looking at her with the exception of one time their
eyes had met. She never wanted anyone, let alone
Gus, to ever look at her that way again. It had been
a venomous glare that gave her the chills.

*Oh what am I going to do? Dad acts like there
has been a death in the family...like when Momma
died.*

Barbara visited when she could and became more
and more alarmed at Steve's condition until Steve

refused to see her when she came. Clover hadn't told her what had happened between him and Charity. However Barbara called daily to check on him. Then one day she came to the ranch and confronted Clover. "Your dad needs to see a doctor."

"He's not going to go to a doctor."

"Well you better do something, before it's too late."

"I know...I know."

Another week passed. She contacted Pastor Evan, who came out as soon as he could.

"What's going on, Clover?"

"Dad and Charity had a fight about three weeks ago. Charity moved out. He's been very depressed ever since."

"I see." Evan knocked on Steve's office door. There was no response.

Clover moved over and opened it. "Dad, Pastor Evan is here," she stated as Steve raised his head. He hadn't shaved in days.

"Steve?" Evan stated, trying to keep his on emotions under control.

"Come in, Evan," Steve, said through chapped lips.

"Let's have prayer," Clover heard, as she closed the door.

Clover paced back and forth. *I can't stay in the house long, I've have too much to do but Dad comes first...I know, I'll make some coffee. Maybe Evan can convince Dad to drink some.* She busied herself in the kitchen then drank a cup of coffee, as she gazed out the window. She watched Dory slowly roam around the corral. *That stupid horse is even in mourning. Isn't there anything or anyone that witch of a white eyes hasn't affected around here?* An hour passed while she fidgeted with one thing and another.

At last she heard Steve's office door open. Clover hurried to meet Evan as he closed it behind him. "Come into the kitchen, we can talk there," she stated, leading the way. "Would you like some coffee?"

"Thanks, I would." He sat down at the table.

"What do you think?" she asked placing two mugs of coffee on the table and sitting opposite him. "He's scarcely eaten anything for three weeks."

"I wouldn't be concerned about that. He's a strong man. A healthy person can go without food twice as long as he has before it affects their health. However, is he taking fluids?"

"Not enough. I was hoping that you could get him to drink a cup of coffee."

"I'll try. Do you know what happened between him and Charity? He wouldn't tell me."

"Uh...well...there were some things missing and Dad accused Charity of taking them."

He shook his head and took a sip of coffee. "That doesn't make sense. I don't think Charity would take anything that didn't belong to her."

"Uh...so...can you help him?"

"Clover, your Dad is in excruciating, emotional pain. His heart is broken."

Tears came to her eyes. "I don't know what to do...I..."

"Clover, I am going to ask you a question." He

raised his right hand, palm towards her, with his elbow bent. "You don't have to answer me but I want you to think about it and then I want you to decide which way you are going to go."

She looked down at the table. "What's the question?" she asked, barely above a whisper.

He lowered his hand and with both palms on the table and leaned toward her. "How's your relationship with God?"

She was silent for a long time. "Not good, Evan," she said, continuing to gaze at the table.

"Well...Promise me you'll think about what I asked you."

"I will," she whispered.

"Good...getting back to your Dad," he said at last. "Steve's had too many losses, between his parents dying when he was young, Charity's mother leaving him, your mother's death and now losing Charity. I think there is only one thing that would get him over this."

"What?"

"If he and Charity could resolve their differences, I think he would be all right."

At last Clover met his gaze. "I know what I have to do," she mumbled.

"Well if you think you can get them back together, you better try."

She sighed. "I will."

"Good. Give me the coffee. I'll see if he'll drink it."

She poured it, handed him the mug and watched as he went through the living room, knocked on Steve's door, then without waiting for a response, walked in.

Later Evan went to tell her goodbye. "I'm going to leave now. Keep me informed."

"I will. Did he drink the coffee?"

"He was drinking it when I left."

While she went about her duties a plan formed in Clover's mind. She quit early and drove into town.

There was only one hotel that was close to Charity's clinic. Clover was reasonably sure that she would be staying there. She knew the owner and it was easy for her to persuade him to let her into Charity's room. *If I came knocking on her door, she will tell me to get lost.*

Clover didn't have long to wait. When Charity opened the door she jumped before she realized it was Clover sitting in a chair. "You startled me!"

"I'm sorry."

"How did you get in here?"

"Charity, just about everyone in these parts knows my family and me."

"Well, *sister,* you can just march right out of here, now!"

"Please hear me out."

Charity grabbed her by the arm and started pulling her towards the door. "I will not! And besides you have a lot of nerve coming here after what you did."

Clover jerked out of her grip. "Charity, listen to me! Dad's in a bad way!"

That got Charity's attention. "What do you mean?"

Clover told her about his condition and Evan's visit.

Charity motioned for Clover to sit down as she took the other chair in the room. "So you want me to move back to the ranch."

"Yes." Tears came into Clover's eyes and for a minute she was unable to say more.

"You would have to tell him the truth."

"I...know," she croaked out.

Charity heaved a sigh. "You realize that you have caused a lot of pain on both sides. I've been pretty miserable too."

"I'm sure you have."

"Is that all you have to say?"

"Give me time...It's hard for me to...to..."

"Admit that you were wrong?"

"Yes...yes... but.... Charity...I... can't stand to see Dad so depressed. You'd feel the same way if you saw him, I'm sure."

"You're changing the subject."

Clover ignored her last statement. "You come home and I promise that you'll never have any more trouble from me."

"And you'll tell him the truth right away?"

Clover brightened. "Yes right away!" She looked at her watch. "If we left now, we could be home in time for supper. All I have to do is heat up the stew."

"Well okay!"

Clover jumped to her feet. "I'll help you pack!"

Charity parked her truck next to Clover's car and followed her into the house.

"Let me talk to him first." She shuddered. "Who knows, I may not have a home after I tell him what I did."

Charity flashed her, a reproachful frown and

refused to give her any emotional support.

Clover shuddered. "Well here goes."

She slowly entered his office. To her surprise he was standing with his back to the door gazing out the window. He had heard them drive up and he recognized Charity's truck.

"Dad?"

He turned and for the first time in days, she could see hope in his eyes.

"I have something to tell you."

"What?" He asked as he sat down.

She stood and hesitantly, with great difficulty, told him everything. Her heart raced as she watched his expression change from astonishment to red-faced anger. When she was through he glared at her speechlessly for an unbearable length of time.

"Daddy please say something!"

"You have done a despicable thing! I would never have believed that you were capable of such an act if I hadn't heard it from your own lips," he ground out from between his teeth. "You had better apologize to Charity. If you know what's good for you!"

She started backing up then turned around and walked to the door and stopped.

"This is not over, not by a long shot, young woman!" He shouted.

She turned her head and sadly glanced over her shoulder at him just before she opened the door and motioned for Charity to come into the room.

Steve leaped from his chair, raced across the room and pulled Charity into his arms.

"Can you forgive an old fool?" He asked.

"There is nothing to forgive. You didn't know...."
"Oh...daughter!"

A few days later, Clover told Charity that she was sorry for what she had done. She genuinely was.

It was a long time before Steve could forgive Clover but eventually they were at peace with one another.

Clover had a new problem. She was beginning to suspect that Billy had no intentions of marrying her. He had used every excuse he could come up with why they had to wait. She also suspected that he was cheating on her. Billy was gone more often at night and when she would question him about it, he would get angry and accuse her of not trusting him.

Chapter 21

Steve recovered quickly. He and Charity were closer than ever before.

He and Barbara dated intermittently.

Branding season was upon them. Gus hurried over to Steve as he was getting ready to climb into his truck. "Them thar poachers air at it agin. Billy and me found hides in the east pasture."

Billy left to start the branding.

"Well Gus, lets you and I go have a look. Billy can handle the crew."

Steve saddled Midnight and Gus rode Dory.

Bluebells, buttercups and shooting stars graced the pastures. Only a few fleecy clouds dotted the big blue sky. It was hard even for Steve to imagine how this gorgeous country could in six months turn into an equally dazzling but harsh, freezing land, where only the strong could endure.

As they neared the spot where Gus and Billy had found the evidence, they had to cross a little knoll. Suddenly a shot rang out and Steve dropped from his horse!

"Steve! Oh God!" Gus yelled as he jumped to the ground. Blood was slowly soaking up Steve's shirt, right over his heart. Gus trembled as he checked Steve's pulse. To his surprise Steve was still alive. Gus quickly removed his own shirt, wadded it up, slipped it under Steve's shirt and put pressure on the wound, then he grabbed Steve's cell phone and punched out 911. Soon the Flight for Life helicopter was on its way. Each time Gus took Steve's pulse it was weaker. However he decided to wait until Steve was safely on board the chopper to call Steve's family.

At last the chopper landed in a clearing about fifty yards from them and two EMTs hurried over with a stretcher. "He's still alive," one of them said to the other, when he felt his carotid artery. He placed an oxygen mask over Steve's nose and mouth. Then after talking to a doctor, he started and I.V. to replenish his fluid loss. The other man replaced Gus's shirt with a compression bandage "Okay let's get him aboard," he said.

Gus watched while Steve was lifted into the chopper. Shortly they were airborne. Gus called Clover and told her what had happened.

As soon as Clover raced off to the hospital a dark figure, carrying a rifle, slowly opened the back door, cautiously peered around the kitchen and crept into the living room. When he saw Molly vacuuming the rug, unnoticed by her, he quickly slipped back out the way he had come. For the next few days someone was always in the house, so he hid the gun and waited for the right opportunity to arise. Finally he gave up the idea, leaving it where he had hid it.

Clover paced the hall as she waited for a nurse or a doctor to bring her news of his condition. At last a surgeon walked up to her. "Are you Miss Wayne?"

"Yes."

"Your Dad is alive but I can't guarantee that he will recover. Even though the bullet barely missed his heart, he has lost a lot of blood and he is very weak. We are giving him blood by I.V. and will continue to until his blood count becomes normal. He's lucky to be alive."

Clover was numb with pain and fear. "So...uh you're saying that he might not make it?"

"Yes, that's a possibility. I'm sorry."

"How soon will you know, doctor."

"I'd say in a few hours...I'll have the ward clerk call the hospital Chaplain, if you like."

"Okay, thanks."

She watched him leave. Tears rolled down her cheeks. *Oh God! Please forgive me for shutting you out and forgive me for all the evil things I have done! Please, please, please, don't take Dad from me!*

Charity was out helping a prize mare give birth when she got the call from Gus. As soon as she could get away she hurried to the hospital. She rushed into the waiting room. "Clover how is Dad?" she asked when she found her among the waiting crowd.

Clover turned tearful eyes on her sister. "He's alive but in critical condition."

"Oh no!"

Clover told her what the doctor had said.

"How did it happen?"

"No one knows but Gus thinks that a stray bullet hit him. They had gone out to check on some poachers."

Charity's temper flared. "It's time to put a stop to those moochers!"

"You're right. I'm surprised they haven't killed

some of our stock."

"I suppose it'll be impossible for Josh to find out who fired that gun."

"Probably, however he's is going to turn the bullet over to the lab. I think he said it was a thirty caliber. Anyway...if someone comes forward with information or if a rifle turns up at a crime scene, they will be able to check to determine if the bullet that hit Dad came from the same gun."

"It sounds like a long shot."

"True but it's all they have for the time being. They have already searched the area for clues and didn't find anything."

Charity had cancelled her appointments for the next two days. She and Clover moved restlessly about the waiting room for over three hours, sometimes talking and other times reading one of the newspapers or magazines. At last a nurse approached them.

"Mister Wayne is out of danger and has regained consciousness."

"Oh thank God!" Clover exclaimed.

Tears came to Charity's eyes. "Can we see him?"

"Not yet but soon. He needs to sleep. Why don't you get something to eat?" She looked at her watch. "They're serving dinner about now."

"Well?" Clover gazed at Charity.

"Sure why not."   Two days later Steve was moved out of intensive care and into a private room. Besides Josh and Gus, Kerby and Troy Glenn called on Steve a few times. They all expressed their concern about the poachers. All Steve's neighbors were edgy, wondering if one of them would be next, to be hit by a stray bullet.

Charity resumed her duties at the clinic.

It was Molly's day off and Clover decided to clean and straighten Steve's office. While he had been depressed he had refused to let anyone in there long enough to tidy up. She organized his papers, vacuumed and dusted the room. Lastly she used Windex on his gun cabinet. Suddenly she realized that something was wrong. Every since she could remember every slot had been occupied with a gun. But now, she saw that one slot was empty. *His thirty-thirty deer rifle is missing!* She called Josh and told him. He came out and dusted Steve's gun cabinet and office for fingerprints. Unfortunately Clover had removed all prints from the cabinet, when she cleaned it.

"Whoever took Dad's rifle probably wore gloves, right?" She asked Josh before he left.

"Probably."

A week later Steve came home and it wasn't long afterwards that he was back on the job. He was angry, when he found out that his rifle was missing. Josh suggested that whoever shot him might have used his own gun. Steve didn't want to believe it, because it meant that someone who had access to the house had tried to kill him.

Time passed and no gun was found that matched the bullet that had injured him. Josh didn't have much hope that they would ever find the gun.

The poaching had stopped. Perhaps what had happened to Steve scared them off.

Chapter 22

"You know Dad; Dory's faster than any other horse that I have ridden. It would be interesting to see just how fast she is," Charity stated at the dinner table one night.

"Are you saying that you would like to have her clocked?"

"Well, yes or see what she could do in a race."

Clover looked up from her plate of spaghetti. "I'll bet she's not any faster than my bay, Ginger."

"Hah! Dory would leave Ginger in the dust!"

Clover gave Charity a long derisive stare, before she answered. "Ginger could easily out run Dory because I would be riding her. I'm the better horsewoman."

"You might be the better horsewoman but Dory's the better horse."

"Hey you two," Steve interjected. "There's one way to settle this. Let's have a race."

"Yes! That's a great idea, Dad," Charity expounded.

Clover flashed Charity a superior look. "I'm game."

"We'll have to agree on the spot and set up some rules," Steve stated.

Clover looked from Steve to Charity. "We could race from the corral to the west hay barn and back,"

"Sounds good to me," Charity stated.

"Let's go look it over after you finish eating, I think it's about three miles, from the corral to the hay barn." Steve downed the last of his tea and waited for his daughters.

Soon all three met at the corral, each on their own mount. "Now remember, this isn't a race. We are going to travel at an easy pace."

"We know Dad," Clover answered impatiently.

It was a beautiful evening. The sun was hovering well above the horizon and wouldn't be down for at least an hour. The birds were still active. A dove cooed. A robin chirped. A crow flew from one pine tree to another, caw...caw...caw, he scolded. The only other sounds were the thud, thud, thud of the horses' hooves as they struck the sod and the occasional squeak of saddle leather.

They all dismounted when they arrived at the west hay barn. "It's not too rough a ride. Someone can drop a handkerchief at the corral. When you get here, you race around the barn and back towards the corral. I'll tie a cord from the corral to the pine tree that's about twenty feet away. Whoever hits the twine first, wins," Steve stated.

Charity smiled at her dad. "Okay by me."

"Fine." Clover said, emotionlessly.

Steve leaned against the barn. "I think you should do some practice runs separately."

Charity moved over next to Steve. "You're right."

Clover nodded.

"When do you want to race?" Steve asked as he sat on the ground

"I'm pretty busy right now but Doc. Ross is going to be on call for me weekend after next. How about that Saturday?"

"Suits me," Clover stated, climbing back on Ginger.

The other two stood, brushed the dirt off their pants and mounted their animals.

Charity told Josh, Clover told Billy and Gus, Steve informed Kerby and soon all their circle of friends including some casual acquaintances knew about the impending race. Then the news spread throughout the community.

Steve acknowledged that there would be betting. He didn't like it but he realized that he wouldn't be able to stop it. Most of their neighbors bet on Clover to win but Gus put his money on Charity. He knew how fast little Dory was.

One day Gus had just finished cleaning the stables when he saw Clover and went over to her as she was putting a saddle on Ginger. "Lo, Missy," Gus stated in his typical gruff manor.

Clover turned around and smiled at him. "What's up, Gussy?"

He flinched but ignored the name she had called him. After all he had dubbed her Missy, since before she could walk. "Air ya going ta make a pracktice run?"

"Yes but I'm sure I don't need to. I'm only doing it to appease Dad. I know that Ginger and I will win the race."

Gus studied her through squinted eyes. "What if ya don't win, Missy?"

She laughed. "Really, Gussy, do you think that little city girl is any match for me? I was practically born in the saddle."

He shook his head. "Ya don't know Dory."

She laughed again. "Ginger will easily outrun that

crow bait. Besides I'm the better horsewoman."

Gus didn't speak while she finished getting Ginger ready to ride. He followed as she led her horse out of the stable. "I think yar in fir more hurt, Missy."

She stopped and looked at Gus. "What do you mean?"

"Dory's likely the fastest hoss on this here ranch, likely the fastest in this here county."

She laughed again. "Oh come on, Gussy, really."

"I'm serious. Ya disremember that I've ridden er."

She scrutinized him for while before she spoke. "I know you're wrong."

"But what if'n I'm right? How ya going ta handle hit?"

"Gussy, there's no way that Charity could outride me, so I'm not going to think about it."

"Ya better think about hit. What I'm tryen ta say is, be ready ta lose."

She gaped at him, at a loss for words.

"Ya toten a heap a jealousy, anger en hate." He put his arm around her shoulders. "Please, my Missy, get shuck of it, afore it eats ya up."

She didn't move, instead she stared at the ground.

"Do ya know, at there air a whole bunch a folks in this here world who'd give thar eye teeth ta have a brother or a sister. Well ya have a sister. And she's a goodun. A sister hat you ken be proud of...Please, Missy. Don't throw hit away."

Clover continued to look at the ground. He removed his arm and walked away.

Steve was aware that a lot of people would show up for the event. He was able to recruit the aid of the other ranchers, who agreed to send some of their ranch hands to help control the mob.

Both girls took their trial runs.

When the day came the weather fully co-operated. The race was to start at ten a.m. sharp. The spectators started arriving around eight. Soon every available parking spot around the house was taken and the vehicles begin to line up down the driveway and out on the county road.

Steve stationed men on horseback, about a quarter of a mile apart along the racing trail. He wanted to be sure that both of his daughters would be safe. Gus was waiting at the barn. There was a lot of money at stake.

Charity became more nervous as the time approached. She didn't know how Clover felt and she wasn't about to ask.

Shortly before ten the sisters lined up in front of the cord. Someone had brought a boom box and the refrains of soft favorites from the eighties permeated the surroundings. Charity glanced around at the assembly. She saw Josh, Cal and Troy together. She caught Josh's eye and he tipped his hat. For some strange reason, the gesture gave her courage.

At ten Steve held the handkerchief up and the audience hushed. The only sound was the boom box. He and his daughters had rehearsed the routine, so they knew that he would count to three and drop the kerchief. Charity held her breath. "One, two, three," Steve shouted. Both horses leaped forward. The crowd hollered and whistled. Then a hush came over them.

The girls were neck and neck when they reached the first station. Steve kept informed with his cell phone. "Neck and neck," he yelled to the crowd, who immediately started to roar. After that he could barely hear what he was told as the race progressed, so, from then on he didn't advise the observers. The girls were still tied when they reached the next station. It continued to be a tie when they reached the hay barn but Clover was on the inside and she took the lead.

"Come on girl, come on!" Charity yelled at Dory, who seemed to understand, accelerated and came abreast of Ginger. However by the time they had reached the next station, Ginger had again taken the lead. Charity didn't push Dory. She knew her horse from the many hours that she had spent in the saddle, so she waited and saved her strength for that last spurt of energy. Ginger continued to stay about a length in the lead. When they reached the final quarter of a mile, Charity urged Dory forward and she didn't disappoint her. Dory took off like a shot, leaving Ginger to eat her dust. When they reached the cord Dory was about three horse lengths ahead. Josh had video taped the finish and later gave it to Charity. The crowed roared and gathered around Charity. Someone threw a lei of yellow and orange chrysanthemums around her neck. Strangers started hugging her. They kept closing in on her until she felt stifled but she continued to treat everyone politely. She spotted Josh as he worked his way through the throng. He handed her a large bouquet of red roses. All she managed to say was thanks before someone else moved in.   She saw Steve standing on the periphery, beaming. Much later he was able to congratulate her with a big hug and present her with a silver charm bracelet that had different types of horses attached to it. Each one was engraved with the word 'Winner.' It was a long time before she could take care of Dory and give her much deserved praise and rub down.

Afterwards she found Clover, who actually was a good sport. She took Charity's hand and congratulated her. "Well Charity, it seems that not only do you have the best horse but you are the better horsewoman."

"I don't think that I'm the better horsewoman. It's just that Dory is so fast...Why don't you ride Dory sometime, and I'll take Ginger and we'll race, privately?"

Clover looked Charity in the eyes. "You'd let me ride Dory?"

"Why not?"

Clover looked down at the ground. "I don't know...It's just that...I've been so rotten to you...I..."

Charity sighed. "Let's forget the past and start over."

Clover met Charity's gaze head on. "I'm not sure that I can ever accept you as my sister."

"You don't have to. But we can be pleasant to each other. After all we are family."

"True."

Clover was nicer to Charity but she didn't act like a loving sister. Surprisingly they started riding together and Clover taught her about the wildflowers and birds. One day Clover rode Dory and Charity Ginger. They raced down the same path as before. Clover and Dory won.

The long summer days were waning. A slight nip was in the air. Charity felt a little sad. To her surprise she had thoroughly enjoyed the long leisurely rides that she and Clover had taken. Of course they would still be able to ride together but less and less as the days became colder and shorter.

Chapter 23

Charity and her staff stood outside her clinic and watched as the parade passed by. The Grand Marshall led on a pinto pony followed by the mayor and his wife in a 1965 Mustang convertible. Next Josh, on a buckskin, led the sheriff's posse. He tipped his hat to her as he came near to where she was standing. Charity's heart missed a beat as she thought about how much she loved him. As he turned his head the sun reflected in something on his hat and she felt shock waves go through her. *Oh my God, his hatband is decorated with silver studs! And He's our sheriff!* The rest of the parade was a blur to her. Later at the clinic she tried to concentrate on her work but in between patients, she would dwell on what she had seen. *I'll tell Dad as soon as I can.* She didn't know where Steve was so as soon as everyone left, she called his cell and told him about Josh's hat.

"So what are you driving at, Charity?"

"I think I forgot to mention that the man, who started the range fire, was wearing a hat with a band that reflected in the sun."

"Charity, there are dozens of western hats, with hatbands that have silver studs on them. More than one of my ranch hands, have hatbands like that."

"Well I guess I got excited for nothing."

"That's okay, daughter. I'm glad you're observant."

Then she remembered overhearing Joe, talking to one of her clients about hunting and a feeling of dread gripped her heart. She recalled him saying that he liked to hunt but that so much of the land was privately owned and that they weren't about to share their hunting rights with the peons. From then on she listened to him and watched him closely for any thing that might connect him to the attacks on her dad.

She and Josh had been dating regularly since they went to the banquet together. Josh had seldom touched her except to hold her hand as they walked together. His attitude amazed her. She was use to the city fellows, who expected bedroom privileges after the first date or at least by the second. *Maybe it's the country code, whatever, it's refreshing.* He started attending Evan's church and afterwards he would go out to lunch with her and Steve. When Josh was a child, he had made a commitment to serve the Lord but when he became a teen he had drifted away from the church, mainly due to the influence of his peers. One Sunday he rededicated his life to God. Charity and Josh talked about how she felt about her mother. He was understanding and encouraged her to discuss the issue with Evan. Eventually she did.

In time, Charity wanted to be in Josh's arms. So one fall day, after they had walked hand in hand out through the back pasture and stood silently absorbing the crisp air and viewing the autumn colors, she turned to him and standing on her tip toes she kissed him. Fire surged through her veins as he returned her kiss with intense fervor. His arms felt warm, safe and perfect. They kissed several times. She was euphoric.

As the days passed they spent most of their spare time together.

"Cal and Troy have gone deer hunting," he said one day while they were having their usual coffee.

"Don't you hunt?"

"No I don't own a rifle." He took a swallow of coffee. "I think Dad was a little disappointed that I couldn't get interested in the sport."

"Does Cal usually get his deer?"

"Most of the time he and Troy go out every year."

"Do I hear wedding bells?" Clover asked one night at dinner.

"Uh...well..," Charity mumbled.

"Yaw...what's up, Daughter? Are you keeping a secret from us?" Steve asked, gazing intently at her.

"If you must know, he hasn't asked me."

"He will...he will."

Chapter 24

Every since Charity had made Montana her home she had wanted to go on a cattle drive but she had been too busy at the clinic, so when the fall drive was about to begin, she got Doc Ross to stand in for her. She could feel the excitement mount as the day approached.

Because Charity was going along Steve decided to make it a camping trip. The cattle had already started down to the lower pastures. Lou, Nat, Hank, Doug, Steve, Charity and Gus left the lazy *W* at six am.

Billy said that he had a bad case of the flu and rather than spread to the rest of the men, Steve decided that Billy should stay at the ranch and try to recover.

The sun was just peeping over the horizon. Each equestrian transported their own food, water and a sleeping bag. Steve carried his rifle on his saddle. What Charity didn't know was that the other five each had a pistol in shoulder holsters, under their coats. Steve had anticipated possible trouble and had taken precautions. He was sure that the saboteur would soon figure out that they were on guard. He thought that knowledge would discourage him from acting. Mainly he wasn't taking any chances with Charity's safety.

A dark figure followed them from what he thought was a safe distance but Steve and Gus had spotted him as soon as it was light enough to see. Steve knew that the perpetrator might try to stampede the herd into the camp while they were sleeping or bushwhack them or try to do some other form of mayhem. Gus especially was wise to such things.

Their horse's hooves, the squeak of leather and occasional conversation between the riders were the only sounds in the crisp morning air until Steve got their attention. "That's a herd of pronghorn antelope," he told Charity as he pointed them out. All the riders reined in their horses and watched them as they grazed. "How interesting," Charity expounded. Their tan and white bodies and short pointed horns were different than any other animal of the deer family that Charity had seen. Only two of them looked in their direction.

Soon the riders moved on. The magnificence of the leaves on the bushes and quaking aspen, of orange, yellow and gold were breathtaking. A white tail doe lying in the grass raised her head as they approached then leaped up and bound away into a grove of cedar trees. Slowly they moved toward the Little Belt Mountains, their silvery, white peaks shining brilliantly in the sun.

At noon the group rested and ate their lunch near some pines. Chipmunks hiding in their branches scolded them for the intrusion. They didn't bother with a fire. As Charity ate she watched a gray squirrel dash along the ground and up a tree, his cheeks bulging with pine nuts.

In early afternoon they reached the herd and set up camp east of them. It was a superb sight to behold. The bulls milled throughout the throng but the calves stayed close to their mothers. The resonance of them could be heard for miles around as they communicated with one another.

Steve sent four of the guys out to round up the strays. Charity rode Dory from one place to another and observed the action. Every now and then she could hear one of the men yell, "Hey, hey, hey, get out of there," as he was flushing out a stray.

The men worked until dinnertime and took turns at the fire, to eat and rest. There was someone on guard at all times. When darkness fell upon them an owl in a tall pine tree periodically hooted,

Lou started playing a guitar and most of them joined in singing songs, such as Home on the Range, Sweet Betsy From Pike, Get Along Little Doggies, My Home's in Montana and In the Land of the Shining Mountains. However during this time Hank and Doug kept circling the herd and watching for danger.

The onlooker cursed when he realized that they were prepared for trouble. He had been in enough cattle drives to know that it wasn't customary for the hands to carry guns but he also knew that under the circumstances they were all armed. His plan was not only to scatter the herd to the point that it would take weeks to find them all, but to drive them through the camp, thus killing Steve and Charity and as many of Steve's boys as possible.

Later Steve had Charity bed down by him, away from the camp on a little knoll in a thicket of bushes, putting her out of danger. Only then did he explain what the others already knew. "But everything is under control, so I don't want you to worry."

"What you're saying is that you're expecting someone to stampede the cattle?"

"Yes but we are well prepared."

He had put her at ease. She could hear the lowing of the cattle, an owl and coyotes as she drifted off to asleep. She had no way of knowing that during the night, each of the men had taken turns guarding the herd.

The villain had no way of knowing that there wasn't anybody sleeping in the camp. Empty sleeping bags had been laid out to look like most of the crew was bedded down.

Just before sunup, the desperado made his move. He had carefully scrutinized Lou and Gus's routine, as it was their watch. They were tired and both appeared to be nearly asleep in their saddles. Shrewd old Gus had expected the villain to strike at daybreak. So when the perpetrator, unaware that the camp was uninhabited, come riding out from a copse of trees shooting, the startled cattle started running in the direction of the camp. However the rest of Steve's men raced out of the darkness from the north, firing their guns in the air and tried to head them off. But the frightened cattle gained momentum. Closer and closer they thundered toward the camp. Tension rose as Steve's men attempted to turn them around. Even though they all wore bandanas covering their noses and mouths, they choked on dust and visibility was at a minimum. However just before they reached the camp the men were able to turn the lead cow toward the south and the rest of the herd followed. Gradually they slowed the bellowing cattle down until they came to a stop. When the perpetrator realized that he had been out maneuvered, he got away in the dark, only because the hands were all busy calming the herd. At that time Steve left the men to finish the job and went back to check on Charity.

She awoke with a start when the first shot was fired. She was a little frightened when she became aware that she was alone. Later when Steve rode in, she ran to him.

"Dad...Dad, I heard gun fire and the roar of the thundering herd." She was shaking.

"It's okay, daughter. It's all over now. We had to turn them. That's why you heard shots."

"But I don't understand. How did you know ahead of time that someone might try to spook the cattle?"

"Gus and I spotted a lone rider yesterday." He held her until she was calm.

"Oh Dad, who do you think he was?"

"I'm not sure, but I think he's the same person who put the black cohosh in the hay and started that range fire."

"You're probably right, Dad."

"Anyway the excitement is all over now."

"What time do you think it is?" She asked at last.

"About five. Why don't you climb back into your sleeping bag and try to rest for awhile."

"Okay."

As soon as she got warm, she blissfully dozed off.

The sun was just above the Little Belt Mountains when she was awakened by the bustle in and around the camp and the aroma of coffee. With the events of the early morning behind her, she recognized that for the rest of her life she would hold the memory of that fantastic Montana morning in her heart. It was not only the mooing of the cattle, the chirping of the birds and the clean fresh air but it was having shared it with her dad which meant so much. When they were drinking their coffee they had smiled at each other and they both knew, without saying a word that they were participating in an unforgettable experience.

Chapter 25

Two weeks before Thanksgiving, Jean was again their houseguest. Steve had insisted that she stay through Thanksgiving. Love swept over Charity for her mother when they embraced but she still hadn't forgiven her. It could have proved awkward if Barbara hadn't decided to spend Thanksgiving with her parents in North Dakota. They all enjoyed evenings in front of the fire.

"As you can see, Jean, life here is not as hard as it use to be," Steve stated one late afternoon, when they had all gathered together and were drinking hot chocolate.

Charity searched her dad's face. *What's he building up to?*

Later Steve and Jean spent time together discussing numerous subjects from politics to religion.

Following Jean's departure, Steve's heart ached for her. For days he fought the urge to call her. *Wise up, Wayne, she's not going to give up her life in California.*

He knew that he wouldn't marry Barbara. As they strolled through her back yard, he gently told her how he felt.

She met his gaze. "Steve I could see this coming."

"You could?" He asked, taken aback.

"Yes, ever since Jean left, you've changed."

"I'm sorry."

She continued to look him in the eye. "Steve, you

love her. For heaven's sakes, do something about it!"

"But...I don't think she'd live in Montana."

"How do you know, unless you ask her?"

He didn't answer her right away. Instead he gazed off into the distance. "Well...I...don't..."

She pulled his cell phone off of his belt and handed it to him. "Call her."

"You don't understand. She left me before. She might do it again."

"Steve none of us know what the future will bring. Life is full of changes."

He closed his eyes. "I know you're right."

"Make that call," she said as she walked toward the house.

It was Saturday. She might be at home. He found her name on his phone and pressed it before he had time to think about it.

His heart sped up, when she answered the phone. "Hello"

"Jean."

"Is that you, Steve?"

"Uh...yes."

"Well, this is a surprise."

"I know...Uh do you think that you could live in Montana?" He blurted out, before he had time to think.

"What are you trying say?" She asked after a pregnant pause.

"I love you, Jean...!"

"Oh Steve, I never stopped loving you!"

He swallowed hard. His heart raced faster. "Oh Jean, come home."

"I'll be on the first plane that goes to Montana!"

"You mean that!"

"Definitely!"

"What about your job?"

"They will just have to do without me."

"We'll have Evan marry us, as soon as he can."

"If you say so."

"I say so, sweetheart."

She was momentarily speechless.

"Jean, are you still there?"

"Uh...yes...I can't think straight."

"Me neither."

"Uh... I'll call the airport to get a flight out, then call you back."

"Wait, you'll need my number."

"I have it."

"You do?"

"Yes...you see I programmed it into my cell phone, over a year ago."

"How did you get it?"

"From Charity's phone."

"Why didn't you call me?"

"I started to several times but I chickened out... By the way how did you get mine?"

"The same way."

She laughed.

"One question."

"What's that?"

"Are you absolutely sure that you could live in Montana?"

She didn't waver. "Absolutely!"

He hesitated. "You won't leave me again?"

"Never!"

On Monday he met her plane. They embraced for some time. She sighed after they kissed. "Oh Steve, it's been so long!"

"Too long." He shook his head. "It's been too long."

Arm in arm they went to get her luggage. "Did you tell the girls?"

"Uh...not yet. I thought we could do it together."

She chucked. "You're as big a coward as I am."

"Probably." He grinned.

Clover was astonished when Steve entered the kitchen, followed by Jean and even more astonished when he told her the news. After she recovered she hugged her dad then Jean.

"I must say you're taking this well," Steve stated.

"I want you to be happy, Dad."

He hugged her again. "Thanks, Daughter."

Unexpectedly Charity reacted differently. She gaped at her dad then her mother. At last she spoke. "But Mom, you don't like Montana!"

"Charity, I do now. It's different then it was twenty years ago."

"I don't see how. It gets just as cold."

Steve cleared his throat. "Let's you and I go for a ride, Charity."

She looked bewildered. "Why?"

"Come on." He took her by the arm and led her out the door. Silently they climbed into his truck

"Where are we going?"

"You'll see."

He drove behind the house and started down what had once been a wagon road. It was rough, the truck bounced and swayed as he drove, so he had to creep along. They passed through a grove of trees and into a clearing where a century old two-story farm house stood. "This is where I grew up and the house that I brought your mother to when we were married."

The old building was overgrown with weeds and brush. The once white paint on the siding was chipped and cracked. The stone path to the house was nearly covered with dirt and grass. The door was stuck and Steve had to butt it with his shoulder to get it to open. It took awhile for their eyes to adjust to the dusky interior but at last she could see an ancient rock fireplace against one wall. "This was our source of heat for this part of the house." The floor was covered with worn black and white linoleum. The walls were paneled pine that had been added sometime in the nineteen-fifties.

She followed him into the kitchen. Green, dilapidated cupboards with doors barely hanging from rusty hinges took up three walls. A cast iron double sink rested in one of the counters. A large black wood cook stove stood forlornly on bent iron legs. The stovepipe had long since collapsed leaving patches of soot on the counters and floor. "All our meals were cooked on that stove and it also heated the kitchen, so in the winter a fire was kept burning all the time."

Fastened to the wall next to the stove stood a tall, rusty, silver cylinder. Pipes were attached from it to the stove.

"What is that?" She asked pointing to the cylinder.

"It's a water tank. Those pipes from the stove heated the water."

"Didn't you have electricity?"

"Yes." He reached up and pointed to an overhead chain that hung from an empty light socket, which was secured to the ceiling. "But only for light. There's one of these in all the rooms."

She looked around. "No plug-ins?"

"No."

"How did Mom iron?"

"We had flat irons. She would have to take turns heating them on the stove."

"Didn't you have a radio?"

"Battery operated."

"Then you didn't have a television."

"No."

"Mom called it the winter from Hell."

"It was. Gus and I and the other hands were gone most of the time trying to keep the stock fed and things going. When I was home I was too tired to stay awake. She had to take care of everything here. I didn't realize that her being a city girl would make any difference. She wasn't use to the hard ranch life, let along the weather. This place was behind the times. I had plans for a new house but it had to wait until I could build up the ranch. Back then I took it for granted that she would understand. When she tried to tell me, I thought she was just spoiled. If my mother had been alive she might have made me understand but it was just your mom and I. She was lonely. There were no close neighbors, no one to talk to during the long hours I was gone."

He took her by the hand and led her to the first

floor bedrooms. There were two, side by side. The same old linoleum covered the floors but the walls were covered with wallpaper, in a faded, rose pattern. It was hanging loose in places. "We had to keep the doors open in the winter to let the heat in from the fire place...Let's go out back."

"What about up there?" She motioned toward the staircase.

"It's not safe. The stairs are rickety and the floor isn't stable either. There's two bedrooms up there just like the ones down here," he stated as they stepped out side.

In the back yard weeds nearly hid a clothesline that had fallen on the ground. Three weather beaten outbuildings stood beyond the clothesline and looked like a puff of smoke could blow them away.

Then she saw a sawed off stump, about eighteen inches tall, with cut marks on top. "What's this?" she asked.

"That's the chopping block, where your mom had to chop the wood to keep the fires burning."

"But didn't you chop the wood?"

"When I could but remember what I told you about that winter. I wasn't there to chop the wood."

"Well I am surprised that you forgave her for leaving you anyway."

"Charity, I'm surprised that she forgave me. I was a real dunderhead."

She was quiet for a little while. "I'm having a hard time forgiving her for lying to me about you... and that's another thing, how can you forgive her, for not telling you about me?"

"Well, Charity, we all make mistakes, do things

148

that hurt other people, besides the Bible says if we don't forgive others, God won't forgive us."

She looked stunned. "Really?"

"Yes, we are all sinners. We are born into sin."

The next Sunday, Evan preached on forgiveness. "Turn in your Bibles to Mark chapter eleven, verse twenty-five. "And when you stand praying, if you hold anything against anyone, forgive him, so that your Father in heaven may forgive you your sins."

Charity made a commitment to serve the Lord. Steve and Jean were delighted.

That afternoon at two o'clock Steve and Jean were married, in the chapel. Gus was the only person who was present that wasn't family.

The following day the newlyweds flew off to Palm Beach, Florida for two weeks in the sun. With Billy's help Clover ran the ranch. Molly and Charity shared the cooking chores.

Chapter 26

Several inches of snow had fallen during the night. Steve had risen early and plowed out their driveway. The snow banks were at least three feet high on either side of the roads.

It had been a slow day at the clinic. Charity had gone Christmas shopping and returned. Julie was reading a magazine when the phone rang. It was Teddy. He was hysterical.

"Teddy, Teddy calm down. I can't understand you."

"Mommy its Benny...he's...he's!"

"Teddy what's the matter?"

"I can't...." He was sobbing uncontrollably.

"Okay son, I'm coming right home." She hung up the phone.

What's the matter?" Charity asked as she walked toward the desk.

"I don't know but Teddy's very upset. I need to run home." Julie put on her coat and gloves and reached for her purse.

"Sure no problem," she said as Julie went out the door.

Charity busied herself with some cleaning chores and Joe went to tend the boarded animals.

Soon Julie came back carrying a badly injured, unconscious Benny in her arms. Tears were running down her cheeks. Teddy followed her. His little face was pale. He was crying softly.

"Oh God, Charity, please help him!" Julie cried.

"Oh...bring him back!"

Joe took the injured animal from Julie and placed

him on the examining table.

"He's barely alive. I think his back is broken but I'll know for sure after I take some x-rays," Charity stated after she examined him. "What happened?"

"Oh no!" Teddy howled.

"Joe," Charity stated. "Take Teddy into the waiting room."

Without a word, he picked up the sobbing child and carried him away.

"What happened?" Charity asked Julie again, as she was getting Benny set up to be x-rayed.

"As far as I could figure out, as Mom, Dad and Teddy were all talking at once, was that dad backed over Benny with the tractor," she stated as she helped Charity with the dog.

"Was he plowing the driveway?"

"Yes. He was almost finished. Teddy had let Benny outside. That dog is crazy about Dad. I guess Benny just wanted to go see him. He bounded off the porch and ran over to where Dad was, just as Dad backed the tracker up to do the last little bit. He didn't see Benny behind him and he ran over him." She wiped her eyes with a tissue that she pulled out of her pocket.

"He's not suffering as long as he's unconscious," Charity explained. "You should go and stay with Teddy. I'll come and tell you as soon as I know something."

"Okay."

"Send Joe in here." She said, as she watched Julie leave.

Joe arrived shortly "He's pretty bad, Charity," Joe stated as he assessed the injured animal.

"Yes he is. I don't think he'll make it, Joe."

Joe heaved a sigh.

After she read the x-rays, she called Julie back and had Joe go to Teddy.

"I'm sorry but he can't recover. His injuries are too extensive. He not only has a broken back and a fractured skull but both of his front shoulders are shattered. I doubt that he will regain consciousness but if he does, he's going to be in a lot of pain."

"Oh no!" Julie whispered. "I don't know how Teddy is going to deal with this. And Dad, he's going to be sick."

Charity put her arms around Julie. "The best thing we can do for Benny now is to put him down."

"Oh Charity, how am I going to tell Teddy!"

"Do you want me to do it?" She asked pulling back and looking in Julie's eyes.

"Would you?"

"O course." Charity called Joe and Teddy back into the examining room, where Benny was laying on the table.

Teddy started petting Benny. He was crying softly. The scene was heart wrenching.

Charity went to him and put her arm around his shoulder. "Teddy, I know you love him very much."

"Yes," he said with a sob.

"I also know that you want what's best for him, right?"

He nodded his head.

"Well, honey, he's not hurting right now, okay?"

Teddy nodded again.

"He's been injured real bad, Teddy."

Teddy caught his breath and looked up at her with

pleading in his eyes.

"Honey, I wish I could say that he is going to get better but he's not."

"No...no!" Teddy sobbed loudly.

"The kind and loving thing to do for Benny is to put him to sleep permanently." She put both of her arms around him and held him close to her. Julie came over and put her arms around both of them.

Teddy continued to sob for some time with his head tight against her. She patiently allowed him to grieve.

At last he turned his tear-streaked face up to her. "You know best, Miss Wayne."

That broke her heart. "Aunt Charity to you honey." She kissed him on the forehead. "You tell me when you're ready for me to put him to sleep."

"Okay."

"You see, all I have to do is draw up a syringe. He won't feel anything."

"It's not going to hurt him?"

"No honey."

"Okay, Aunt Charity."

Charity caught Julie's attention and nodded her head, to the side, twice. Julie understood and took Teddy back to the waiting room. Then Charity prepared the syringe that ended Benny's life.

For several days afterwards she felt like a member of her own family had died.

Chapter 27

Two weeks before Christmas, Josh took Charity to an elegant restaurant. White table clothes and bowls of floating red and white candles enhanced the tables. Swags of evergreen branches and multi-colored, blinking Christmas lights decorated the walls close to the ceilings.

They both ordered filet mignon.

Charity's heart was full. Her family was complete at last. Clover treated her with respect but not with love. She was glad that Clover hadn't done anything to hurt her mother. She had obviously learned her lesson well. And Charity knew that Clover loved their dad a great deal and wanted him to be happy.

"You have literally beamed lately, Charity." His voice sounded deeper and gravellier than usual.

She reached over and took his hand. "Yes everything is right in my world right now. It means so much to me that my mom and dad are back together. What gives me the most joy is that I have forgiven my mom for not telling me about my dad."

"I bet they are both pretty happy."

"They act like a couple of lovebirds. Sometimes it's a little embarrassing but I'd rather have them like that than fighting."

He grinned. "You're right."

Their meal arrived and they chatted about their occupations and laughed over some of the humorous things that happened to them lately. When they finished eating, the waitress brought them more coffee and cleared the dishes away.

He nervously started talking about how much they

had in common and how compatible they were. Charity was amused, as it was the most words that she had heard him say all at one time.

"Josh, what's the matter?" She asked when he stopped to take a breath.

"Uh...well don't you think we're...uh compatible?"

She was fairly sure that he was going to propose. "Of course and we love each other."

He swallowed hard. "Right."

"So go ahead and ask me," she said gently.

He gave her a long look that made her heart race. Then he reached into his pocket and pulled out a black velvet box. "How did you know?"

She threw him an astute look. "What else?"

He didn't get down on his knees and she was relieved. She didn't want an audience.

When he opened the box all she could say was, "Oh!"

The wedding ring was a simple platinum band but three Marquise diamonds rested in the filigree, on the engagement ring.

"Will you marry me?"

"Yes! I will."

After he slipped the engagement ring on her finger he pulled her to her feet and kissed her. Suddenly the other patrons started to clap. They had an audience after all.

Steve, Jean, Clover and Troy Glenn were in the kitchen playing scrabble when they went to tell them about the engagement.

Troy had become more and more attentive towards

Clover, in the last few months.

"We have news." Charity beamed.

"I bet I can guess," Clover, said looking perceptive.

"Me too," Troy exclaimed, grinning.

"Well I think we should give them a chance to tell us," Steve stated.

"By all means," Jean added in support.

Josh took a hold of Charity's left hand and extended it so they could all see the glitter of the diamonds under the lights.

"How pretty!" Jean interjected hugging Charity, then Josh.

"It's lovely, Charity," Clover stated.

"Congratulations," Troy added and shook Josh's hand.

Steve hugged Charity than took Josh's out stretched hand. "Yes, congratulations...There's no one else who I would rather see marry my one of daughters than you, Josh."

"Why thank you Steve."

Clover hugged Josh then Charity. "I hope you will be very happy," she said sincerely.

Charity was touched. That was the first time that Clover had hugged her.

"When's the wedding?" Steve asked.

"We haven't decided yet. I guess when we can both get away." Charity stated.

A few days later, Josh picked her up in his truck. "Cal took my car. He and some of his friends are going to Butte to a mineral show. There wasn't enough room in the truck for all of them."

She and Josh went to dinner, then drove around

and looked at the Christmas lights and decorations. When they arrived back at her ranch, he opened truck door and the light came on. Her purse was on the floor. When she bent down to get it, she spotted a rifle under the seat. Her heart froze. That's when she remembered him saying that he didn't hunt and that he didn't own a rifle.

Somehow she got through the last minutes of goodbyes. But when she was alone in her room her imagination ran wild. *What if it was he that I saw start the range fire? After all he has a hat with studs on the band.* She started to undress. *If he could get Dad to sell out at a low price, he would own the biggest ranch in western Montana. Then if I was his wife, our children would be the heirs and he wouldn't have to share with Clover. Maybe...Just maybe he and Joe are in it together. Joe would have an opportunity to plant the cohosh in the hay. He's been to the ranch on numerous occasions with Doc Ross and with me... And maybe later when the sabotaging hadn't worked, Josh had decided to shoot Dad. It would be easy to pin it on the poachers. And becoming sheriff fit right into his plans, because anything suspicious that happened would be reported to him.* She didn't sleep that night. She was looking out her window when the sun came up. *If I told Dad what I suspect, he wouldn't believe it. I wish there was someone I could talk to.* For the first time she wished that she and Clover were close. It would be nice to have another woman besides her mom to confide in. *Mom...that's it! I'll talk to her about it!*

That evening when she returned home from the

clinic, Steve was still out tending to his duties. She found Jean in the master bedroom, rearranging her wardrobe. "Well, Charity, what's on your mind?" She asked, looking surprised.

"I have a problem and I need to talk about it."

Jean sat down on the bed and motioned for Charity to sit beside her. "Now what is this all about?"

Charity told her what she suspected with tears in her eyes.

Jean put her arm around Charity's shoulders. "Why don't you tell your dad?"

"Because I'm sure he won't believe that Josh is involved." She told Jean what his reaction had been when she had informed him about the hatband. "I can hear him now... Having a rifle under the seat doesn't mean a thing. Lots of guys have rifles under their truck seats."

"Well...I tell you what. We'll pray about this and just wait. I know it's going to be tough but you need to give Josh the benefit of the doubt. You love him and trust is important in a relationship."

She turned to Jean. "Thanks Mom." They embraced and she kissed her. They had become close again, only it was better.

An ad in the Sunday paper caught Charity's eye. 'Adorable registered black Lab puppies for sale.' She called the number listed. They had one male left. He was the runt of the litter. She rushed over to buy him. Then she called Julie and told her about him.

"I'll bring him over on Christmas Eve, okay?"

"Oh Charity. That would be wonderful!"

When she arrived at Julie's house her dad and

mom were there.

"I have something for you Teddy," she said sitting box down on the floor in front of the little boy.

"What is it, Aunt Charity?" He asked soberly, Teddy wasn't the jubilant child he had been before Benny died.

A whimper came from the box. Teddy's green eyes light up and he clamped his hand over his mouth. Charity opened the box

The puppy started jumping up and down and yipping. Teddy squealed with delight and picked the Lab up and held him close. There wasn't a dry eye in the room.

The little boy's joy returned. Benny the Second and his little master from then on were inseparable.

Chapter 28

The Christmas holidays were behind them. Charity hadn't seen much of Josh, as they had both been quite busy. They had grabbed a few minutes here and there, at the coffee shop or on the phone. The extreme cold was hard on the range animals and she and Joe were averaging around twelve hour days. She was seriously thinking of taking on a partner. Josh also had a heavy load as he was investigating the murder of a farmer. A suspect was in custody but there were many aspects to the case that required his attention. And someone wearing a ski mask had robbed a country bar and dance hall. No one had been arrested for the crime. Josh had spent many hours running down leads.

One evening as they were about to close the clinic down for the day, Joe went out back to dump the trash. Charity hollered at him that there was a bag of old papers and magazines that needed to be thrown away but he didn't hear her. Charity reached for the bag and stepped out to dispose of it. To her surprise about thirty feet down the alley, Joe, with his back to her, was talking to Josh, in low tones. Josh was leaned up against his truck. They hadn't seen her. She hurried back in side. *They certainly appeared chummy. It seems strange that neither one have ever mentioned the other one to me.* Her heart sunk. *Besides if Joe hates big ranchers, why is he being so congenial with Josh?* She didn't ask Joe about what she had just seen.

Depression nearly took control of her. That evening she told Jean what she had seen. Jean gave her wise counsel. "Things aren't always as they appear."

"But Mom, what if Josh and Joe are working together to get this ranch? Shouldn't we talk to a Federal Marshal or the FBI?"

"First of all, I think it's time to talk to your dad about this."

"But Mom I don't think he'll take it seriously."

"It's worth a try. He's the one who has the most to lose, possibly his life. I tell you what, I'll talk to him."

She groaned. "Okay Mom. Please let me know what he says."

They embraced. "I will."

Later that evening, Steve called Charity into his office. Jean was already there, standing to the side of his desk, when Charity entered the room. As Steve sat down behind his desk, Charity took a chair and Jean sat in the one next to her.

"Your mother told me about your suspicions."

"Dad I'm very disturbed about this!"

"I know you are. But I want you to know that it's under control."

"What do you mean?"

"You're right about one thing, there is something getting ready to happen. But don't talk to anyone else about this."

Her heart started to pound. "Dad if you know something about Josh...I mean he is my fiancé...!"

"Daughter, please don't worry about this. It's going to be all right, I promise."

"But Dad what if someone tries to kill you? What if it wasn't a poacher or a stray bullet that nearly killed you last fall?"

"Charity, trust me. No one is going to try to kill me."

"How do you know, Dad?"

"I know because the law is about to move in on the perpetrators. But promise me that you won't breathe a word about this to anyone."

Charity heaved a sigh. "Okay, I promise."

From that moment on she tried not to think about the issue and buried herself in her work

Chapter 29

The general opinion among the ranchers was that Basil could get up to one hundred thousand dollars at an auction. Steve wasn't convinced that he was that valuable but he knew that he owned the most productive stud in the county.

It was after mid-night and very dark when a van moved down the county road, stopped and the driver switched off the headlights. His companion stepped out of the truck, took a flashlight and led the way as the driver turned the truck around and slowly backed it toward Basil's pen, which was about three hundred yards from the house. When the vehicle reached the pen the two men worked together to lower the ramp. They walked through a layer of crisp snow that crunched with each step. Then one of them used a bolt cutter and severed the chain that was attached to a padlock. Silently they approached Basil. One of the men slipped a halter on him and led him to the van. Suddenly floodlights illuminated the area. One of the men stood still while the other, although blinded by the lights, pulled a pistol out from his coat and started firing wildly. Someone fired back and he grabbed his shoulder and ran to the truck and jumped in. He gunned the motor. Gravel flew up as the van raced away. The ramp bounced around noisily as it drug on the ground. When it neared the county road, a sheriff's car pulled out of the darkness and in front of the van, blocking the way. The driver of the van backed it up, shattering the ramp, then sped forward and rammed the sheriff car pushing it out of the way. The van then raced out of sight.

"He won't get far," Josh told Steve. "We have roadblocks out about two hundred yards, both ways." Josh punched out a number on his cell phone. "Yaw, Jake, he's headed your way. He's armed. Shoot his tires. I'll be there in a jiffy."

Steve shook Joe's hand. "You did a good job, setting him up."

The shots had awakened Charity and Clover. Jean, who knew what was happening, was already awake. All three jerked on their robes and ran toward the lights. Charity was the first lady to arrive on the scene. "What... happened?" She asked breathlessly, as she looked at Josh, Steve then Joe.

"I have to go," Josh stated and stepped into the shadows where his car had been hidden. Soon he sped away in a cloud of dust.

"What's Joe doing here?" Charity asked. At that moment Clover ran up to them followed by Jean.

"Joe is our hero. He was collaborating with Josh to catch our saboteur."

"Really, you mean he was working undercover?"

"Yes, he met him in a bar a couple of years ago and the two started drinking together. The first time the saboteur got drunk, his tongue loosened up and he said that he was going to be getting a big piece of land soon."

"At first I didn't think too much about it." Joe stated. "I thought it was booze talking but each time that we got together, he would reveal a little more to me. What got me to wondering if he was the fire starter when he said that some big rancher was going to give him a portion of land, when this

164

rancher could buy out another big spread, at far below the market value."

"So who was the saboteur?" Clover asked.

"I'm sorry to tell you this but...Billy has been scheming behind my back. Josh is sure that he planted the black cohosh in the hay that caused several of my breed cows to abort."

Clover gasped.

"And he's the one who shot Steve," Joe stated.

Clover's temper flared. "That dirty, rotten, filthy...Oh!" She raised her arms, with her elbows bent and her fists clenched.

"He also tried to stampede the cattle into our camp, during our last cattle drive. But let's continue this conversation in the house," Steve stated, after he put Basil back in his pen.

Clover raged all the way to the house. "He's a big phony! He pretended to love me. He even said that he wanted to marry me! Oh!"

"Aren't you glad that you didn't marry him?" Charity asked.

"Oh! God yes! You know, I doubt that he ever wanted me. What he wanted was our land!"

"Do you remember that about six months ago Jack's Bar and Dance Hall was robbed?" Steve asked the others, after they were sitting around the dining room table.

"Yes," Charity stated. "The crime was never solved."

"Well, shortly after the robbery, Billy suddenly had extra cash."

"You see Billy has a big gambling problem like his father before him and he was pretty far in debt."

Joe stated. "Then all of a sudden after the robbery, he had enough money to pay it off."

"But if Billy were dishonest, why would he care if he paid his debts or not?" Charity asked.

Joe raised his eyebrows as he gazed at her. "Those guys he owed the money to play rough. Billy knew enough not to rile them."

"So who is the big rancher that is behind Billy?" Clover asked.

"Josh has a fairly good idea but he's not saying, not until he can make an arrest" Steve stated.

Clover thought for a moment. "Dad, there's only four other ranchs that border ours besides Jordan's...Glenn's, on the north side, and Kelly's, Melbourne's and the Johnson's on the east!"

"I know. It makes me sad to think that one of our long time neighbors could be greedy enough to want to see me dead, to gain more land."

Steve's cell phone buzzed. "Hello."

"Josh, here, Billy pulled a fast one. When he saw the roadblock, he backed up, turned around in your driveway and went the opposite way. He busted through the other roadblock."

"He has an advantage over you. He knows every inch of this country."

"Not really, Steve. You see Joe put a tracking device on the van and I'm right behind it."

"That's good, Josh."

"I'll let you know when we have him in custody."

"Okay thanks, Josh."

He told the others, what Josh had said.

Jean brought coffee. Everyone took a steaming hot mug.

"Charity," Joe said. "You remember that I was knocking the big ranchers and other successful people?"

"Uh...Yes."

"It was all an act. I had to make people believe that I was a jealous jerk, so I would be convincing for Billy. As it was, it took a long time before he began to trust me and let me in on his plan to steal Basil."

"What was he going to do with Basil?"

"He had a buyer in Idaho who was willing to give him fifty thousand dollars for him. But he was also going to send Steve a ransom note and of course by the time ransom was paid, Basil would be long gone."

"You see if I had paid the ransom and lost Basil also, it would hurt me a great deal financially. I might not have been able to recover." Steve interjected.

"So, whoever was after the ranch might be able to pick it up for below the market value."

"Right."

"What were you suppose to gain from helping Billy steal Basil, Joe?" Clover asked.

"Ten thousand dollars, one fifth of the ransom money."

"Wow! That's a lot of money for a few hours work... and Joe, I'm glad that you're honest and were willing to take a risk."

"Yes, the Wayne family owes you our deepest gratitude. Actually you deserve a reward."

"No...no. I don't want money from you."

"Is there anything you would like?"

"Well now that you mention it...uh..."

"What, Joe?" Steve asked.

"Actually it's Charity who could help me."

"What?" She asked.

"I've wanted to be a veterinarian for a long time. I've saved up the money but I need someone to sponsor me."

"Consider it done."

Chapter 30

Billy's right shoulder ached. His shirt and the inside of his coat were soaked with blood. He had to steer with his left hand. It was awkward enough with both hands, on the winding country road. *I'll take the Jackson cut off and dump the van. I can hide it in back of the barn, at the old Jackson ranch. It's only a mile from there over to Dub Bakers. I'll grab his Harley. He always leaves the key on the doorframe of the shed. It's at least four hours before daylight. He won't miss the bike until later this afternoon. That should give me about a sixteen hour head start.* Beads of sweat clung to his forehead and neck. His wound had temporarily coagulated. *Brown set me up! I should have known better than to trust him.*

Billy turned the van sharply to the left onto the Jackson cutoff.

Josh went past the road then backed up and followed the van.

The road was rough and the pain in Billy's shoulder was excruciating. He grimaced each time he hit a bump. Every twist of the road became more difficult.

Josh was careful to stay back far enough from the van so Billy wouldn't spot him.

Billy slowed down and turned into the abandoned Jackson ranch. The lane to the old barn was little more than a path and was even rougher than the road he had just passed over. He nearly passed out from his throbbing wound that had opened up again. He could feel the warm, thick liquid run down his chest and soak into the waist of his jeans. *Got... to find a way... to stop the bleeding.* Billy maneuvered the van down the old wagon trail that went around to the back of the barn and out of sight of the road. When he shut off the motor he heard the sound of Josh's car. His heart started to pound. Although he was very weak from the loss of blood, Billy was tough and had great inbred endurance. He climbed out of the truck and slipped into the dark, moonless night. Few people knew of the back trail that went from the Jackson ranch to Dub Bakers. Billy had been over it several times.

Josh hurried to the van and scanned it with his flashlight. He pulled his cell off of his belt. "Hello Steve, Josh here. Billy's gone off into the night. It's too dark to follow him, even though he's leaving a blood trail. I don't think he can get far. He's got to be pretty weak."

"Don't underestimate him, Josh. He's tougher than most men. Besides there is more than one trail out of there and he knows them all."

"Well do you have any ideas?"

"Yes, he's going to need help. Billy will likely either contact the rancher that he's been working with or his grandfather."

"That's what I thought, I'll put a tail on the rancher and have his place staked out."

"If I know his grandfather, old Charlie Hawk Claw, he won't help Billy if he thinks he's guilty. But blood is thicker than water and Billy can be a convincing liar."

"I think I'll head up to Charlie's place but I won't let him know that I'm out there watching the place."

"Okay. Keep me informed."

"Will do." Josh hooked his cell back on his belt.

Billy hadn't gone far when, with great difficulty, he pulled out his shoelaces. Then he took off his coat, placed it on the ground, pulled his pistol out from under his belt, laying it on his coat and took off his shirt. Billy tied the laces together, wrapped them around the left side of his neck and under his right arm. He bunched up the area of his shirt that wasn't stiff with dried blood and pressed it tightly against the wound and tied the laces together in front, holding the compress securely in place. Then he stuck the pistol back under his belt, put on his coat and leaned against a pine tree to catch his breath and give the wound a chance to re-coagulate. That's when he heard Josh's car start and move off into the distance. He forced himself to move forward but he didn't try to hurry to Dub's place. *I know that I have the advantage for the time being.* About halfway he stopped again to rest. This time he sat down in the snow. *It's not going to melt for awhile; it's too cold out here.* The bleeding had stopped, partly because of the sub-zero temperature. He was very cold but he ignored it. He had more pressing problems.

Finally he trudged on and didn't stop until he arrived at the shed. Billy took a chance and flipped the light on just long enough to check his watch. It was three thirty. He dropped to floor and put his head down for fifteen minutes.

Before long Billy walked the bike down a path. The only sound was the crunch of the snow. He had to use both hands to push the bike and he almost passed out from the throbbing pain in his shoulder. Shortly he came to a bend in the trail and was out of sight of the house when he mounted, started the Harley and took off. It took constant diligence to keep the bike upright on the rough ground. Billy steered with his left hand and in spite of his immeasurable strength he had to steady the bike occasionally with his right hand. Each time the pain grew worse. After one such ordeal, Billy lost consciousness. He fell onto the freezing ground on one side of the trail; the bike went on for about twelve more feet before it dropped to the other side. He didn't know how long he laid there. When he came to, at first he thought he had just woke up from a nightmare but gradually he realized that he was living one. He could hear the bike motor running. Slowly he staggered to his feet. He was colder than he had ever been in his life. Billy's hands were numb and he could hardly grip the handlebars. It took him four tries to upright the bike. Each time the pain ripped through him, like he had been stabbed with a knife. His mind was in a haze most of the rest of the journey.

It was daylight when Billy reached the old shack that he had sometimes stayed in during hunting season. He laboriously, and in severe pain, dragged the bike through the door. Billy didn't allow himself the luxury of a fire for fear that someone might see the smoke and come snooping around. His stomach complained bitterly and he was suffering from hypothermia but he was so tired and weak that he dropped down on the old cot and fell fast asleep.

Besides the cot, a rickety wooden table, a chair

and a pot-bellied stove were the only furnishings in the cabin.

When he awoke the sun, high in the sky, beat down on the tin roof and had raised the temperature inside the shack. His body felt warm for the first time since he had abandoned the van. Besides a box of wooden matches, there was a can of pork and beans, on the only shelf. He opened it with his pocketknife. As there were no utensils, he tipped it up and little by little managed to gulp most of the contents, before scraping the rest out with his fingers. He wiped his fingers on his jeans and then he punched out a number on his cell phone.

"Yaw," a gravely voice answered.

"This is Billy. I'm in trouble."

"I know and you're on your own."

"Hey if I get caught, we both go down."

"I told you before. No one is going to take your word against mine."

"Maybe not but you'll be under suspicion and that could jeopardize your good standing in the community."

"Well like I told you before, you're on your own and don't call me again." The phone went dead.

He cursed and hooked the phone on his belt.

There was a creek about fifty feet in back of the cabin. Billy painfully made his way to the water, rinsed out the bean can and filled it three times, drinking the clear, clean water, before filling it again for future use. Then he washed his knife.

When he returned to the cabin, he checked his wound. It was red around the clot. *I have to get that bullet out.* He started slowly scraping the dried

173

blood off the wound. Fresh blood started to ooze out. Billy grimaced and started probing with his knife. He touched the bullet with the knife but he knew it was next to the bone and in too deep. He was close to passing out again. Finding a clean place on his shirt, he tied it back against the wound.

He slept for a couple more hours. When he awoke, he called his grandfather's number and let it ring for some time. *Where are you when I need you?* He angrily punched the off button.

Chapter 31

Later Billy called his friend Harry, who had been his buddy since they were both kids. They would do most anything for each other. Harry agreed to help him.

Billy dozed off again.

The sun had moved to the western sky when he opened his eyes and was shining through one of the two dirt streaked windows.

Billy was miserable. He was hungry, in pain and feverish. He picked up his phone and punched out his grandfather's number again. Charlie answered after the second ring.

"Lo."

"Hello Grandfather."

"Oh, it's you, Blackbird?"

"Yes...Grandfather."

"Where are you?"

"Uh... I'm in trouble, Grandfather."

There was a pause. "What kind of trouble?"

"I've been accused of something that I didn't do. I ran away and I'm hiding out."

"Why did you run, Blackbird?"

"Because I was shot by the sheriff and he would have killed me, if I hadn't gotten away."

There was another pause. "Listen to me. You shouldn't have run away, Blackbird. Josh Jordan is a fair man. He wouldn't have shot you if you had given yourself up."

"He thinks I'm guilty and no one is going to believe that I'm innocent. Steve's on his side too.

You have to help me, Grandfather...please! I need to get the bullet out!"

"What do you want me to do?"

"I'm sure Josh has someone watching your house. And you will probably be followed, to see if you contact me. Have Bonnie drive you to my friend Harry's cafe and park out front. Harry will give Bonnie the keys to his Taurus. You go out the back door. Take the Taurus and meet me at the State Park...Oh and bring food, I'm starved. I'll have Harry have it ready when you pick up the keys."

"I still think you should turn yourself in."

"Please help me, Grandfather!"

"Well, we'll meet you at the park, anyway."

"Thanks Grandfather. I'll see you soon."

Billy checked the gas tank. *It's half full, more than enough to get to the park.*

Painfully he pushed the bike back to the trail and mounted it. *The ride's going to be brutal but I don't dare risk taking the road. Besides by taking the trail I can cut off about twenty miles.*

If he wasn't miserable, a fugitive and had on warmer clothing, the journey might have been a pleasant one. The air was fresh and clean. It hadn't snowed for a few days, so the trail was passable, however blankets of snow rested between the many pine, fir, quaking aspen trees and juniper bushes along the trail. Unnoticed by Billy, a white tail doe, startled by the bike, stopped eating the bark of a quaking aspen and bounded away into the forest. Along the trail, rabbits, foxes, and raccoons warily observed him pass by.

An hour after he left the cabin he came to the edge

176

of the park, stopped and turned off the engine. It was silent as a tomb. He spotted the Taurus in one of the camping spots, about two hundred feet away. Billy carefully scanned the park to be sure no one else was there. Satisfied, he turned the bike around and hid it behind some bushes. Before he got to the car, Bonnie jumped out and hugged him. Then when she stepped back, she looked shocked by his wet, dirty, appearance. Charlie climbed out of the passenger side and gazed over the car at his grandson. He studied him, while Bonnie handed Billy the food. Then he moved around the car as Billy took a drumstick out of the bag taking a bite. Billy was unable to look Charlie in the eyes.

"You don't look very good, Blackbird," Charlie said at last.

Billy had gulped down the chicken and had started to consume a biscuit. "I know...Grandfather. I need...a bath and...some dry clean clothes," he said between bites. "Let's go."

All three got into the car, Billy in the back. "I want you to take me to the house. The law is likely still at the cafe, waiting for you to come out."

"We need to get that bullet out," Bonnie stated.

"It will have to wait until you take the Taurus back to the cafe and come out the front door."

"Okay."

"We'll get the bullet out and then we'll talk about the right thing to do, Blackbird," Charlie stated firmly.

When they neared the city, Billy lay down on the floor. No one spoke as they covered the twenty miles to Charlie and Bonnie's farm. Bonnie drove into the garage and Billy slipped in the back door. He hid the pistol behind a family picture, on the bookcase. Exhausted he dropped down on the couch.

Bonnie backed out, turned around and headed back to the cafe.

Earlier that day Deputy Ken Ward had replaced Josh at the farm. If Josh had been on the job, they might not have been able to trick him. But the officer had followed Charlie and Bonnie to the cafe, as Billy had hoped he would and was still waiting for them to come out. He started gazing at his watch and was about to go inside and check when they exited the building. He followed them back to their ranch.

Soon, with the help of some whiskey inside Billy, Bonnie was able to remove the bullet. Later after Bonnie got the bleeding stopped, she cleansed the wound with some peroxide and pulled it together with one stitch.

"Billy you need an antibiotic. I've cleaned it the best I can but you have an infection and it's going to get worse," Bonnie stated with concern.

Charlie helped Billy wash up and Bonnie brought him some of his grandfather's clean clothes. He stretched out on the couch and immediately went to sleep. Bonnie covered him with an afghan.

Unnoticed Charlie put the bullet into his pocket.

Chapter 32

"Blackbird, we have to talk," Charlie stated after Billy sat up and pushed the afghan to the side. Charlie's aboriginal face was deeply lined. Bonnie kept his short, white, thick hair neatly trimmed. In spite of his advanced years, his eyesight was still excellent.

"Sure, Grandfather."

"You say you're innocent but as long as you stay here, you're a fugitive. I want to call Josh and tell him that you will surrender to him." Charlie's black eyes scrutinized his grandson.

"No, please Grandfather, don't do it!" Billy still would not look Charlie in the eyes.

"But if you're innocent, you have nothing to worry about."

"I told you that Steve, Josh and all of them are against me. I don't have a chance. Please Grandfather let me stay here a few days and then I'll go away."

Charlie sadly shook his head. He put on his coat and sat outside on the porch. Down deep he knew the truth. He had seen the signs a long time ago, little things through the years, like Billy using charm to manipulate people to get out of trouble. He had told himself that sooner or later he would grow up, be a man and quite blaming other people for his problems. He felt partly to blame. Charlie had tried to help Billy over the rough times, when Billy's weak father had lost everything gambling and shortly afterwards his mother had died. But looking back, he realized that he had been too soft on the boy. Instead of allowing adversity to build his character, Charlie had protected him too much; consequently Billy had the attitude that he was special, exempt from what everyone else had to face.

The old man had overcome many hardships. He had been born on a dry and bleak reservation. His family had barely survived. It was a sad existence for a once strong and brave people, who before their defeat had been free to live off the land, in lush green, fertile, valleys and rolling hills that provided them with plenty of wild game for clothing and food. An abundance of berries, nuts, roots and herbs had supplemented their diet. The old ones had often talked about those former days. He could only imagine what they were like.

Charlie had gone to the white man's school, had listened to the counsel of his mother and wisely taken the white man's ways. Thus in time he was able to integrate and eventually buy a farm. Ironically it was on some of the same land that his ancestors had once freely roamed. However Charlie wasn't bitter. He had accepted his way of life.

Finally with a heavy heart he slowly went back into the house. Bonnie was busy in the kitchen and Billy was reclined on the couch watching television. Unseen, he took the phone into his bedroom and called Josh.

Sometime later as prearranged, Josh and Ken parked their car out of sight of the house and carefully edged their way toward the house. Bonnie was working at the kitchen sink when she glanced out the window and spotted movement in some bushes near the back porch. She dropped the knife that she had been using into the sink and rushed into the living room. "Billy, somebody coming!" Hurry, go out the back bedroom window! I think they have the doors both covered!"

Billy leaped to his feet, grabbed the gun, knocking the picture over, raced through the house and out the window, closing it behind him, unseen by either lawman. Bonnie put the picture back in its place and hurried back to the kitchen. When Ken came through the back door without a sound, Bonnie, knife in hand, looked appropriately startled.

Charley was sitting on the front porch waiting when Josh silently climbed the steps and slowly opened the door. Gradually each man worked his way toward the living room. They were both surprised that Billy wasn't there. "He must have gone out through a window." Josh stated after they had searched the house.

They both rushed out the back door. "He couldn't have gotten far. He's on foot." Josh stated. "You go that way." He pointed north. "I'll go east. We'll circle around and see if we can pick up his trail."

Billy was weak and feverish. After his surge of adrenaline wore off he could barely drag himself along through the tall quack grass and bushes. He didn't have time to cover his tracks and he knew if he didn't think of something quickly Josh and Ken would catch up with him. Then he remembered a cedar tree that he used to climb when he was a kid. It had a crook in it that was big, fairly comfortable and was well hidden in the branches. When he and Bonnie use to play hide and seek she was never able to find him up there.

He could hear someone following him when he arrived at the tree. He picked up a branch off of the ground, went back about forty feet and used the branch to destroy his tracks. He dragged it behind him until he got back to the tree. His strength was about spent. He tried three times before he could grasp the trunk of the tree and barrel walk up it. Sweating profusely, he was almost to the crook, when he started sliding back down. The bark dug into his arms, tearing the flesh. He had to let go and he hit the ground with a thud. He lay there temporarily hidden in the grass, conserving his strength. Presently he heard someone passing on the other side of the tree. As they moved away, Billy exerted all his energy and tackled the tree once more. Unbelievably he made it to the crook but his head was spinning and he wondered if he would be able to stay there. He straddled the crook and lost consciousness.

Some time later when he came to, he could hear movement below him. Gazing through the branches he saw, Josh, Ken, Bonnie and his grandfather.

"He has got to be around here. He was here on the ground." He pointed to the area where Billy had flattened the grass, earlier.

Dang, if I hadn't crushed the grass, they wouldn't have stopped here. He watched as Josh and Ken searched all around the area. Bonnie sat down on the ground but Charley stood. *I know that sign. He's pondering and that's not good for me.* Billy pulled a cone from a branch and threw it as far as he could, in his weaken condition. All but Charley went in the direction of where the cone had fallen. *Dang it, Grandfather, why can't I ever fool you?*

After the others had thoroughly searched and returned to the tree, Charley caught Josh's eye and pointed with his thumb, up to where Billy was hiding. About then Ken saw Charley and started to climb the tree. "He's up here alright!" He hollered as he neared the crook.

With some difficulty, Billy was able to get his pistol out from under his belt. He fired but his shot went wild. He was shaking violently from weakness and fever.

Ken dropped to the ground, unharmed.

"Billy drop your gun! You can't kill us both," Josh yelled.

Bonnie darted under the branches where she could see Billy's face and started to scream. "Don't Billy! Stop, please!" Tears were running down her cheeks.

Billy cursed and fired another shot first at Josh then at Ken, missing them both. His grandfather stepped in front of them.

"Blackbird, my boy, give me the gun."

"No!" He put the pistol against his temple. "I'm not going to jail!"

"Billy don't!" Bonnie screamed.

He was so weak he could barely hold the gun against his head. "I'd rather die then to be locked up," he mumbled.

Josh moved to where he could see Billy. "Think of your grandfather and Bonnie. Do you want to hurt them even more then you have already?" Josh pleaded.

He didn't move for a time but like a trapped

animal, his eyes wide with fear, darted back and forth from Josh to Bonnie and his grandfather.

"It's hopeless," Billy said at last.

"There's always hope, if you're alive, Billy," Josh responded.

Billy closed his eyes, lowered his head and dropped the pistol to the ground. Slowly he started to climb down. When he was in reach, Josh moved forward and eased him to the ground. He staggered and would have fallen if Josh hadn't steadied him. "You're feverish, Billy. You need medical attention," Josh stated as he clapped handcuffs on him. Ken picked up Billy's gun.

Charlie and Bonnie followed them and watched as Josh led him away and put him in the back of his vehicle.

Chapter 33

"You have a visitor, Blake. The deputy stated and watched Billy roll over, away from the wall and sit up on the edge of the bunk. "Who is it?"

"A lady."

Billy's eyes widened when he saw Clover and the fury in her eyes. He didn't speak.

"You dirty rotten scoundrel! You tried to steal our land!"

He poured on the charm. "Now, baby. A man is innocent, until proven guilty."

"Don't baby me, you villain! And save the charm. It doesn't work anymore."

"But, baby, we love each other. You're my gal."

"I'm not your gal! And I don't love you. The man I thought I loved was decent and honorable. You're not that man!"

He stared at her long and hard. At last he knew she meant what she said. He squinted his eyes and screamed at her, "Get out of here, you dumb little country hick!"

She glared back at him. "Aha! The real Billy comes out of his cage!"

He was enraged. "I'm going to be found innocent on the grounds of entrapment and I'll be a free man. And I'll get you for this!"

She threw back her head and laughed at him. "You stupid idiot, there's too much against you. You'll probably get life in prison."

He sneered at her. "For trying to steal a bull?"

"No for attempted murder. You tried to kill my dad, you louse!"

He was silent for a moment. Then his mouth twitted in a grin. "Now who's going to prove it?"

She didn't answer him. Instead she turned and left him.

He had been pretty sure, when he had consulted with his lawyer, that he would get off because of the entrapment thing but now he was beginning to get uneasy. *Maybe the law has more evidence than I thought and maybe, when I was drinking with Joe, I talked too much....Joe that dirty stool pigeon!*

Clover remembered that Billy had a storage closet in the stable. She told Josh and Steve about it. All three of them went to see what was in there. It was secured with a padlock. Steve got a screwdriver and removed the latch. Inside a travel case sat in front of a long overcoat that hung from a hook. Josh took the coat down and there against the back of the cabinet was Steve's gun. Josh whistled between his teeth.

"My rifle!" Steve expounded.

"Yes and when we run a ballistic test on it, I'd be willing to bet that this is the gun that nearly took your life!" Josh put on his gloves and reached for the gun. "I need to check it for fingerprints but I'm sure that Billy had sense enough to wear gloves."

"More than likely."

Josh opened up the bag and pulled out a black ski mask. "Did you know that the man who robbed Jack's Bar wore a black ski mask?"

Billy's lawyer convinced him that it would be best for him to plea bargain, so Billy named the rancher who had put him up to all his evil deeds. At first Kerby Glenn tried to talk his way out of it. "I had nothing to do with what Billy is accusing me of. Surely you're not going to take his word against mine," he stated smugly. "Why I hardly know the boy. We don't travel in the same circles." However as careful as Kerby had been, his son Troy had seen Billy and his dad parked out together, on a country road a few times and he wondered about it, so when Kerby was brought in for questioning, Troy told Josh what he had seen.

When Billy's trial came up, the courtroom was packed with the locals. Billy wasn't popular because he was accused of harmful attempt toward and trying to kill one of their leading citizens. There was so much booing and sneering that the judge had to clear the courtroom.

Billy got twenty years, with no chance of parole or getting off for good behavior.

Kerby Glenn died of a heart attack before his trial date was set.

NINE YEARS LATER

Joe made it through veterinary school and became Charity's partner. She was glad to be able to spend more time with her husband Josh, seven year old Josh junior and five year old Jean.

Clover married Troy Glenn and lived at the Glenn ranch with their three children.

The families have often gotten together, especially for birthdays and holidays.

Steve retired and travels a great deal with his wife Jean. However they return periodically to visit their daughters and enjoy their grandchildren. His foreman Earl competently oversees the Wayne ranch.

Teddy Harris for the first time in nine years was separated from Benny the Second, as he had gone off to college and was taking pre-med.

Twelve years later Charity clipped an article from the local paper that read: 'Theodore Harris MD, an Osteopathic Surgeon, has just returned to the city to set up his practice.'

One of his first stops was to see his Aunt Charity.

THE END

24462851R00107

Made in the USA
San Bernardino, CA
25 September 2015